A KISS IS JUST A KISS

Book One of the Love & Kisses trilogy

Nicholas Scott

A Kiss Is Just a Kiss

By Nicholas Scott

Copyright 2014 Nicholas Scott

26 Letter Productions

2nd Edition

DEDICATION

They say love comes in many forms and we learn to love from those around us. We learn everything from those around us. M.J. taught me the meaning of love, what it is to love, what it feels like to be loved, the desire, the yearning to love someone. Everything before was a notion; everything after, a steady evolution.

CHAPTER ONE

First Kiss

"So yeah. I just want to try it." Aiden Pike was an Adonis. Simply put, one of the most beautiful guys I'd ever seen. And he knew it, not that *I* thought he was beautiful, but that pretty much *everyone* thought he was beautiful. How we had become friends in the last couple of weeks is a mystery to me. I'll admit I had a sneaking suspicion that there was some sort of bet going on behind my back, à la Cruel Intentions.

"Let me get this straight. You, Mr. Popularity, Mr. I-Can-Have-Anyone-I-Wanted, you, want to kiss me, Cody Beaumont?"

His smirk was to die for; that mouth, those lips, beautiful and mesmerizing.

"Well, I normally just go by Aiden, but yeah, I want to kiss you." He grinned devilishly, leaning against the wall, his nicely sculpted abs peeking out from between the bottom of his t-shirt and the top of his jeans.

"Why me?" Don't get me wrong, sure I was cute, but in comparison, well, there was no comparison.

"Why not?" He countered casually. He stared directly at me, his eyes boring into mine.

"Sweet talker." I meant it to come out stronger, but the words tumbled out, a choked whisper, losing the irony I intended.

Aiden rolled his eyes. "Hey, it's a win-win situation."

"Win-win?"

"Yeah" Aiden put a hand on his chest. " Look, I know." He took a step closer. I tried to look away but he had me mesmerized. "I've seen the way you look at me." He leaned forward and whispered, his breath tickling my neck, his lips grazing against my ear "You practically rape with me your eyes."

1

I blushed. It was true. I couldn't count the number of times I'd undressed that boy in my mind. It didn't help that he had no modesty, none whatsoever. The first time we hung out, this was like right before classes started up again and we were over at my apartment. He was slumming it. The complex has pool and he wanted to use it. Why, I don't know, because his was Olympic size. I had to force him to put on a pair of my swim shorts. Course that didn't stop him from dropping trow, right in front of me, not a care in the world. And by the end of the afternoon, he was swimming buck-naked while I was walking around with a giant towel wrapped around my waist, hiding my excitement.

"How about this. You let me kiss you and I'll let you suck me off. Y'all like that sort of thing."

I didn't know whether I was suddenly excited or pissed off. "Y'all?" I looked at him, incredulous. *He did not just say that!*

"Yeah fa." He stopped himself as I quirked an eyebrow. "Come on, you know what I mean." He tried to laugh it off.

"First off, you arrogant prick, the fact that you're asking *me* to kiss *you* is pretty fucking gay. Second, believe me when I tell you, if I were to suck you off, not only would you like it, but you'd be begging me to do it again and again."

"Hey I'm just asking you for a favor and giving you something in return." My boastful bragging seemed to have no effect on him.

He took two steps back and had the audacity to pull his t-shirt off. His abs were perfectly sculpted, the definition so exquisitely chiseled, I couldn't help but stare. His arms, shoulders, chest; they were all flawless. I was actually drooling. I swallowed, searching my suddenly bloodless brain for a retort, a quip, any sort of witty reply that might negate my jaw dropped reaction to him.

"You want me Beaumont. And you can have me, just this once, for a kiss." He undid his jeans and let them puddle around his ankles. He was going commando.

"Come on!" I croaked. This was not happening.

He reached across the two steps between us and took my hands pulling me closer. He placed one palm flat against his chest. I could feel his heart beating, slow, steady and strong. He took a deep breath then guided my other hand to his cock. I felt it growing, hardening in my grasp. "One kiss." He teased. It was just a whisper. Reaching behind me, he untucked my shirttail and rolled the shirt up, as well as the ribbed tank top underneath.

This was not happening. I kept saying it over and over in my head, but was unable to speak the words aloud.

He was fully erect in my hand as he wrapped his own around mine, his big palm warm. Slowly he began thrusting in our grasp. A glistening bead of precum seeped from the tip of his cock. He moaned as he rubbed the ball of his thumb across the sensitive head.

With a skilled hand he finessed my jeans open and let them drop. He slipped a hand inside the waistband of my Calvin Kleins and I shuddered as he deftly sent tremors quaking through me.

In my wildest of dreams, I couldn't imagine anything more erotic, more sensuous. I leaned into him, relishing his excitement, desperate to give in to his request. His lips glistened and I wanted nothing more than to taste them. He slid his hand around the base of my neck and drew me into the kiss.

I couldn't help but wonder if he'd done this before. It was a foregone conclusion that he'd been with girls. There were stories and at least one illuminating iPhone video to validate his heterosexuality, but the ease at which he yielded to the kiss, the eagerness at which he accepted my tongue; there was a familiarity to his actions that seemed too natural. I couldn't help but wonder about the sex. Being impaled, feeling his weight on top of me, his teeth biting me, his fingers digging into my hips. I moaned into his mouth as he kissed me hungrily.

The kiss was over before I knew it. I stood motionless, my face upturned, breathless. Aiden's eyes were closed and to me, he never looked more vulnerable. I leaned in to kiss him again.

CHAPTER TWO

Kisses Interruptus

"I said one kiss. One!'

Aiden had his hands on my chest keeping me at arms length.

The scene, from the outside, had to look ridiculous. Aiden was completely naked, his rigid cock, which just seconds ago was stabbing me ever so gently in the balls now pointed up at me at an inviting forty five degree angle. My hands clasped his shoulder, my arms straining to pull him back to me for another kiss.

"Seriously?" I struggled to pull him closer. Damn my weak upper body strength. "Have you seen you? You're like a wonderfully chiseled, perfectly ripped *NAKED* Lays Potato Chip. I can't just have one!" I don't know where the food analogy came from; I just know I wanted more.

"Look." He used a fancy wrestling move and rotated me around to where my backside was pressed against his front side and my arms crisscrossed my chest like I was wearing an invisible straight jacket. I'd like to say I struggled to get free, but to be honest, I liked how everything was feeling at the moment and any struggle on my part was for the friction. Two can play at this game. He tried to maneuver his groin in a less opportune location, but I thrust my ass back against him.

"Damn it Beaumont. Stop!" He was breathing heavy against my neck. "You're such an ass."

I nudged backwards again. "How the fuck is it that I'm the ass." I fought to free myself from his hold to no avail. "You all but seduced me with your...with your.... with your nakedness!" I bellowed victorious as I freed an arm, but with the force, my arm flailed back and I elbowed Aiden in the nose. Instantly I was free and stumbling forward, my legs tangled in the jeans puddled around my ankles.

"Son of a bitch. I'm bleeding." A line of blood trickled down Aiden's forearm.

"Hold your head back. Lemme get you a towel. Come on." I grabbed his free hand and navigated the hallway, accidentally bouncing him off the doorframe. "Oh shit. I'm sorry, I'm sorry."

"Mother fucker. Let go. Just let go!"

I let go of him, holding my hands up, placating. I backed up and into the bathroom where I grabbed a washcloth and soaked it in cold water.

He leaned against the wall, knocking a framed photo of the Leaning Tower of Pisa further askew. He looked at me under the arch of his arm as I handed him the washcloth and I was surprised to see him smiling.

"What?"

"Passive aggressive much?"

"I didn't... I mean... " I was flustered. I was frustrated. I was horny as hell.

"Look. Beaumont. I'm not gay. You know I have a girlfriend. I really like her. I didn't mean to come on so strong. I just wanted to know what all the fuss was about."

"All the fuss?"

"Yeah, guy on guy. You know, the gay stuff." He checked his nose to see if it was still bleeding. He seemed satisfied and dabbed under his nose with the washcloth.

"Oh yeah. The gay stuff." I nodded, rolling my eyes at the same time. "For the record, we didn't do any of *the gay stuff*." I did the whole parenthetical bunny ears with my fingers.

"We did!" He insisted. "I mean, I touched your junk." He seemed almost embarrassed to say it.

I leaned against the other wall, smiling. Yes he did. I remembered the sensation, the tremor as he seized my cock.

"Stop thinking about it!"

"Can't" I said it as a matter of fact. "It's stuck there. PESD."

"What?

"Post Erotic Sensation Disorder"

"You're making that up."

"I know." I closed my eyes and pretended to visualize the moment over again. I moaned lasciviously, banging a fisted hand against the wall, licking my lips and gyrating my hips.

"Fucker." Aiden grinned at me.

His erection was gone, his dick hanging. He was bigger than I was and I felt a momentary envy. He caught me staring and covered himself with his hands. He looked down, the washcloth balled tightly in his grasp. "I'm sorry."

"For what?" Had the world gone topsy-turvy? Aiden Pike, arrogant prick, was apologizing to me. Not only that, but showing a modicum of modesty.

"I know you like me. And I'm flattered. I mean, I really like you..." He looked up quickly then amended. "Hanging out with you, I mean."

I nodded, trying my damnedest to smile. *Shit, just stop talking. Just don't say...*

"You're like a brother to me."

It was like he read my mind. Son of a bitch!

"Look, I know what I said. About you sucking me off. If you want..."

I was shaking my head before he even finished the thought. I don't know what was wrong with me. *Cody Beaumont get ahold of yourself, drop down on your knees and get some!*

"Come on. You know you want to."

I squeezed my eyes closed. "I think... I think you need to leave." *Holy shit, did I just say that?*

Aiden pushed himself off the wall and stood in front of me in all his glory. There was nothing intentionally provocative or suggestive in his movement and I struggled not to reach out and touch him, to trace a finger down his abs. Shafts of late afternoon sunlight painted us a golden bronze, but he was idyllic and beautiful and I was mesmerized. He leaned forward then, running the ball of his thumb across my bottom lip then closed in and kissed me again. It was a soft kiss, a sensuous, lovely; a kiss that made me cry. It was the longing, the desire, some deep down need for tenderness that overwhelmed me emotionally. I kissed him back hungrily, groping for him to hold me up. He broke the kiss, leaning back, smiling.

"Okay." I shook my head. "You really need to go. I don't think I could take another one."

CHAPTER THREE

Don't Tell Anyone

"Is that extra caramel on there, too? Ughhhh, you bastard!" Emily was on a diet and under the false impression that I should support her by joining in on her masochistic plight and deny myself one of the few joys of my life.

I sipped my caramel mocha Frappuccino®, moaning excessively. Emily blew absently on her Zen™ Brewed Tea staring daggers at me over the rim of her cup.

"What? It's not my fault you're on a diet. *Again.*"

"Yes! Yes it is. Since you told me about you and," Em leaned in and whispered conspiratorially. "*Aiden.*" *She* looked to her left and then right before continuing. "I've been binge eating. I ate a whole bag of those new potato chips; the ones that taste like cheesy garlic bread. A whole bag! In one sitting."

"Those are good."

"That's not the point, I...." She leaned in again, checking to make sure the coast was still clear. Never mind we were sitting in the corner by ourselves. "I still don't get how it happened."

"I told you. We were hanging out and he said he wanted to kiss me."

"Were you wrestling."

I laughed so hard I nearly choked on my frap. "What! Why would you ask that?"

"Well wrestling is kinda homoerotic." She drew figure 8s on the table with her finger and said in a sing-songy voice. " I mean I hear that's kinda hot. One thing leads to another."

"God. That is so cliché. That's like me asking if you had a pillow fight in your negligee at your last slumber party." I shook my head, stirring the whipped cream into the rest of my frap.

7

"So you had a slumber party? I didn't know guys even had slumber parties? Course it does sound awfully gay, a guy slumber party. I mean…"

"Em. Em." I held a hand up in her face. "Shush and drink your tea.

Emily was beautiful, she was sexy, she was funny, and I loved her to death, but she was not the sharpest crayon in the box. Despite the deep chocolate locks that crowned her head, I had the sneaking suspicion Emily had been a string of natural blonds in her previous lives.

She looked at me suspiciously. "I know what you're thinking."

I nudged my Frappuccino®, across the table in her direction. "I'm thinking…you need a sip of my frap before you go on a tea induced killing spree."

Em grabbed and drank greedily. "Oh my gosh this is so good."

I reached for it but she leaned out of my reach and drank more frantically.

"I said a sip!"

Emily started choking; her eyes growing huge as she stared over my shoulder.

"What?"

I looked back and saw Aiden standing in the entrance. I looked back at Em who was smiling really big, still drinking. *"Oh My God."* I mouthed the words silently.

It had been almost a week since we'd seen each other. I refused to call him, as much as I wanted to and when I saw his name on the caller ID, the one time he called, I ignored it.

"Hi Em. Can I borrow Cody for a minute."

Emily grinned real big, took a final big sip of my drink until the straw made that grating sound. "Sure." She picked up her hot tea again and took a cautious sip. "Mmm. It's just right now."

I stood up and followed Aiden back outside to his car. I loved his car; a red MINI Cooper convertible. He opened the passenger door and motioned for me to get in. It was dark inside the tinted windows. I watched him walk around the front of the car, then get in.

"Your brother told me where you were." He settled into his seat. He nodded in the direction of Starbucks. "You told her?"

I nodded hesitantly then hurriedly said. "She won't tell anybody. I just. I had to tell someone. I'm sorry Aiden."

Aiden shook his head. "It's okay. I... I... if she tells anyone though, we're through."

I nodded. I started shivering. I'd forgotten how cold it was outside, but the cold wasn't the only thing affecting me. I wanted to ask him what he meant by 'we're through.'

Aiden started the ignition and turned the heater on full blast. "D'you tell anyone else." I could hear the anxiety in his voice.

"No. No one else. I swear."

He nodded in response and relaxed back in his seat. "Shit!"

"What's wrong Aiden?" I reached over and touched his arm.

He twitched from my touch.

"Nothing. I just...we shouldn't have done it."

He was all kinds of screwed up. "Aiden. It was just a kiss, remember. Just a kiss."

"Two. It was two kisses. And I touched..." He squeezed his eyes closed as if it was too much to accept.

"Aiden. Seriously. It's not that big of a deal. We're the only ones that know and I swear, I swear, Emily won't tell a soul."

Aiden shook his head and wiped at his eyes.

"Hey." I took his hand "Aiden. Seriously. Are you okay? You're kinda scaring me."

He pulled his hand free and took a few short quick breaths. "Yeah. Yeah, I'm fine. I shouldn't have come." He looked at me and smiled, though his eyes were distant and afraid. "Seriously. I just needed to make sure you weren't going to tell anyone." He looked back over at Starbucks. "Anyone else."

I reddened. I knew I shouldn't have told Emily, but like I told Aiden, I had to tell someone. He took another deep breath. "Okay." He stared straight ahead. I guess that was my cue to leave. I reached for the handle.

"Beaumont?"

"Huh? I looked back at him.

"Please. Don't tell anyone. Not even Emily."

"But I already..."

His lips were warm, his nose a little cold as he pulled me by my jacket into another kiss. He kissed me hard then pushed me away. He reached across my lap and opened my door.

"Okay."

CHAPTER FOUR

Cloves and Orange Liquer

"Damn it." I threw my phone on my bed, unwilling to call Aiden. I told Siri to call Em. "I'm going crazy. We gotta go do something."

t waited a good 35 minutes for Em to arrive and another hour waiting as she sat on the bathroom counter and played with her makeup. I say played because once she was done she wiped it all off. "I think I'm gonna go au naturel." I wanted to strangle her.

"So, what are we going to do?"

I looked at her and she collapsed on my bed. "I thought you knew!" I picked up a pillow, not knowing whether I wanted to smother her or pelt her senseless. I pressed my face into the pillow and screamed.

"Oh my god. You need to get laid."

I hadn't told Em about the kiss at Starbucks. I just told her that he wanted his space. In case you've never experienced it first hand, Emily swears *a lot.* I was torn between being touched by her being so protective and guilty for the fact that I lied to her.

"Oh I know. There's a party. Chloe Hart's parents won a weekend getaway in Bermuda. Chloe was acting like she won it. She's such a bitch. Anyway, she's throwing a party. A few close friends she said, so you know like everybody is going to be there."

I rolled my eyes. It's not that I didn't like parties. I loved parties. I loved parties too much. Parties loved me; especially parties with vodka.

"Em, you know how I get."

She nodded. "If anybody needs to let loose and have a drink, it's you, mon ami. Have a drink, find a hottie and have your way

10

with him. Do a little drunken house cleaning upstairs." She tapped me on the temple. "Forget that fucker."

I winced. It was obvious Aiden Pike was on Emily's shit list. Not a great place to be.

"Come on," Emily was prone to whining. "Em needs a party toooooo."

"Fine. But you're driving. And we're having Taco Bell first. And you have to buy."

Oh Cody, you're the best date ever. Don't expect me to put out." She twirled back to the mirror and grabbed one of the 13 shades of red lipstick she carried in her purse.. "Oh! Cherry Mango." She dabbed her lips on a tissue. "What do you think?"

"They look the same."

"It's lip gloss you Neanderthal. Here..." She leaned into me and held me by the back of the neck and proceeded to gloss my lips. "That's better."

"Better than what? My lips are just fine, thank you." I started to wipe the stuff off.

"Stop. Stop." She slapped at my hands. "Nobody wants to kiss, just fine." She handed me a tissue. "Here. Just dab. I said dab! Don't wipe. Are you sure you're gay?" I took another proffered tissue and mimicked Em dabbing her lips. "Okay, I take it back, you're definitely gay."

I wadded the tissue and threw it at her.

We arrived at the party and had to park almost two blocks away. Getting out of the car, we could already hear the music. I cringed as Em did a little happy dance then looped her arm through mine and proceeded to skip alongside me. "Come on. Turn that frown upside down." She poked herself in the cheek rotating her hand to produce and overly animated and somewhat creepy smile. "We're gonna have some fun if it kills you."

"It just might." She bumped me with her hip, her curls bouncing as she skipped. The girl needed a pill. Or maybe I did.

We threaded our way in and out of partygoers dancing to Avicii's *Hey Brother*. Em squeaked, then smiled abashedly as someone groped her ass. "I like this party already."

"Harlot." I joked.

"Prude."

She seized my hand and dragged me to the kitchen. She grabbed a bottle of cheap vodka and a red Solo cup off a table and poured. "Drink." She commanded. The vodka went down rough and almost came back up. She took the cup again and poured. "Drink." She held it out to me expectantly.

"Can I at least smoke first?" I pushed my way past a group of drunk jocks and out to the patio. A group of emo guys were perched on the patio furniture enveloped in a thick plume of smoke. I knocked a cigarette from my pack of Marlboros and slammed the vodka.

I was already feeling it by the time I finished my cigarette. It was warm and I was pulling at the collar of my V-neck when the blond emo sat down.

"Where'd your friend go?"

"Huh." My head felt heavy and I grinned. I looked around but didn't see Em anywhere.

"Can I have one?" He lifted my pack of cigarettes.

"Sure." I fumbled in my pocket for my lighter and saw Em behind the sliding glass door giving me a double thumbs-up gesture. I flipped her off. She kissed the glass leaving a smear of lip-gloss. I couldn't help but laugh.

"What?" He looked back and I caught a glimpse of the back his neck. He had a beautiful neck. I had a thing for necks. I wanted to touch it; to kiss it. I leaned in and inhaled the scent of him. He turned back around, puzzled. I shook my head, and then upended my cup, getting nothing but a couple of drops of vodka. Blond emo boy pulled a flask out the pocket of his black hoodie. He offered it to me. I took a tentative sniff: Grand Marnier.

I handed it back to him after taking a drink. He had long thin pale fingers, which lingered on mine. I leaned in and kissed him. He tasted of clove cigarettes and orange liqueur. I licked his lips and kissed him again.

"What the fuck!"

Aiden stood in the kitchen. Em stood behind him, her arms crossed triumphantly.

12

CHAPTER FIVE

Run Away

The party was in full swing but starting to deteriorate as parties do when they are a barely controlled chaos. Music roared from the speakers, the bass shaking everything like a sustained rhythmic earthquake. I followed Aiden, weaving through the mash of people in the living room who danced and swayed and grinded to the music. Bursts of laughter shot from different directions. The aromas of alcohol, cigarettes and pot permeated the air comingling with the tangy scents of body odor and lust. I called Aiden's name but lost sight of him.

I was going to kill Em.

I found her sitting with the blond emo boy. He rolled his head, which was propped on her shoulder and looked up at me. His arm rose like a puppeteer controlled it. "I'm Ashton, by the way."

"Cody."

He dropped his head back on Emily's shoulder but kept eye contact. "How do you know Ems?" " I realized he looked like Christofer Drew from Never Shout Never.

"Oh. Ems and I go way back." I looked at Emily. "Ems, can I talk to you for a minute." My smile was tight, my anger barely controlled. I took her hand and yanked her up. "We'll be right back." I dragged Emily under the dark bows of a giant Eucalyptus tree. "You set me up."

"What? He's cute. And he thinks you're cute. " She leaned into me. "He said you're a great kisser." All I could see of her smile was her white teeth.

"He did? I blushed in the dark. "Wait...don't try and change the topic. You set me up!"

"You're welcome." She hugged herself against the cold.

"NO. Not you're welcome. I didn't need to be set up. I didn't want to be set up and and…and"

"And what?" She was feeling triumphant.

"And you showed Aiden!" I shouted.

"He asked where you were. What was I supposed to do, lie to him?" Her voice feigned innocence.

"YES!" I yanked one of the big Eucalyptus leaves from the tree. "I can't believe you did that."

"What's the big deal? He's straight. Not to mention he's got a girlfriend. It's not a happily-ever-after story with him."

I knew she was right. Anything with Aiden was going to have drama written all over it. I peered back through the leaves at Ashton. He had lit another of my cigarettes, trying to blow smoke rings. I watched his lips working, his tongue darting out "So, he said I was a great kisser?"

Emily followed my gaze to Ashton. She smiled. "Yes. His exact words were: "the best kisser." She rolled her eyes. "I probably shouldn't tell you but he's got a huge…"

"Emily!" I covered her mouth with my hand. "And how would you know?"

She pulled at my hand. "A girls gotta eat."

I covered her mouth again. "Nope. I did not hear that". I shook my head as Emily laughed.

She pried my hand away again. "I'm kidding. I'm kidding. Not about his huge," she leaned in, "cock, but about the other thing. He loves the Skittles. I mean, we did make out once, but that's it. He wouldn't even grab my tits." She sounded almost offended.

"Then how do you know?"

"Chance told me."

I nodded. Chance McAvoy was…what's the word…a big ol' hoe. "So he and Chance…"

"No. No. No."

"Seriously Em, just tell me already." I rolled my eyes as we came out from under the tree and headed back over to Ashton.

"Oh. All of the sudden, you're all about someone besides Aiden Pike."

"Well now that you've screwed everything up between me and Aiden…" I found myself absently searching for his face.

"He has a girlfriend!"

We stopped in front of Ashton. He was lying on his back, blowing smoke rings into the air, oblivious of his surroundings. He opened his eyes. "Ems, you're back." He had an adorable drunken lazy smile   He held his hands out blindly. Emily grabbed them and pulled him upright.   He reached into the pocket of his hoodie and pulled out his little black flask. He took a short nip, grimacing as he swallowed then offered it to Emily. He turned to me as she shook her head. I reached for the flask, but he took my hand instead and pulled himself up. "Hi Cody." He draped both arms over my shoulders, leaning into me and pressing his forehead against mine. His nose was cold and I could smell the orange liqueur on his breath. He licked his lips. "You're not gonna run away if I kiss you again, are you?"

Both our heads slowly rolled one way and then the other, as I shook my head. Em was right. Aiden had a girlfriend. He was straight.

"Good." He shot his tongue out for a quick lick across my bottom lip. I held his face in both hands as he tried it again. I captured his tongue in my mouth, and kissed him hard. He crammed a hand in my back pocket and pulled my crotch tight against his own. The other hand was at the back of my neck. He suckled my tongue, nipped at my lips, biting softly, while taking great gasps of air. His kisses were hungry.   "God." He moaned in my mouth.

"Ahem." Emily cleared her throat, hands on her hips.

We both looked at her. She threw up her arms in frustration then disappeared inside the house.

I smile mischievously. Ashton gave me a quick kiss and then a flurry of kisses. His hands traveled under my shirt then down to my crotch. He grabbed one of my hands and shoved it down the front of his jeans

"Come on." He led me through the house, staggering. I hooked a couple of fingers through one of his belt loops.

In the bathroom, he slapped off the lights, hopped on the counter, legs wide, leaning against the mirror. I heard him working his zipper. Then he kissed me.

CHAPTER SIX

Just My Luck

"Wait." I had to catch my breath. But more importantly, I had to lock the door. I reached blindly behind me for the door handle in the dark. Finding it, I pushed in the little button, listening for the metallic click. Ashton took that as his cue and yanked me back. He grabbed at my shirt, pulling it over my head. Then our lips smashed together again. He inched forward and jumped off the counter and pushed me back against the wall, the towel rack digging into my shoulder blade. I yelped in response but Ashton was oblivious as he dropped to his knees, tugging at my belt. I reached down to help but he smacked my hands away and then I felt the belt slip free and clang to the bathroom floor. My jeans were down in a flash and Ashton had his face buried in my crotch, his hands groping my ass. I could only moan in response as he mouthed me through my briefs. I grabbed a handful of his shirt and dragged him back up and into a deep kiss. I pulled at his shirt and lifting his arms, he slipped right out of it. My eyes had adjusted to the darkness. From the light coming under the door I could make out his pink nipples against pale flesh. I leaned in and kissed one and then the other, biting softly. Ashton drove his fingers through my hair. I kicked off my jeans and kissed my way down his chest, tracing my tongue along his flat abs to his belly button. I kissed him there, loving the scent drifting up from his crotch. He was tenting his briefs so I slipped a couple of finger under the waistband and yanked them down. His cock bounced up and slapped his belly button. I grabbed him with both hands and licked the head. He moaned loud enough to drown out the music, thrusting his hips. I grazed my teeth across it and then ran my tongue along the shaft. Ashton squirmed. He was mine for the taking.

The pounding on the door scared the shit out of me.

"COPS!" Someone bellowed.

I screamed in frustration. I don't think Ashton even heard; he kept pawing at me pulling my hair, thrusting his rigid cock in my face.

"Son of a bitch. Motherfucker!" I scrambled back up to my feet and I slapped on the lights and stood dumbfounded as I stared at Ashton. He stood naked before me; a milky white god chiseled of marble. He was flawless and beautiful. The only things that marred his flesh were the teeth marks blooming around his nipples.

We could hear people running through the hall outside the bathroom door. The music had gone quiet and muted voices were yelling. I grabbed clothes off the floor jumping into a pair of jeans that belonged Ashton. I kicked them off and he held mine out to me. We were dressed almost as fast as we had disrobed. Ashton pulled me into a final kiss.

"Get my number from Ems." His fingers lingered on my chin and then he was gone, running into a dark room. I watched several shadows slip out the window while red and blue lights flashed outside.

I slid down the wall, maddened and frustrated. I banged my head on the wall.

"Cody? Cody?" Em appeared in the doorway, her shoes in her hand. She rested her hands on her hips. "Are you drunk?" She can pick the worst times to be motherly.

I couldn't help but growl. "No. As a matter of fact I was about to…"

"OHHH EMMM GEEE. You and Ashton? I thought you came back here after Aiden.

What do you mean OMG? You saw the two of us kissing. And you stormed off. Plus, I couldn't find him." I felt a momentary guilt but I could hear Em's words in the back of my mind. *He's straight. He's got a girlfriend.* If anyone should be feeling guilty, it should be him. He has the audacity to get pissed at me. I shimmied back up the wall and looked at myself in the mirror. My hair was a mess; my lips were chafed and swollen. I had a lip-shaped hickey just above my collarbone and I could tell there was going to be a huge bruise on my shoulder blade.

"I didn't storm off. And I saw Aiden come back here. I just figured..." Em got real quiet and slowly turned her head towards the shower curtain. It was a dark blue patterned art deco that reminded me of The Great Gatsby movie, the one with Leonardo.

I shook my head. Certainly not. What were the chances? Really? I could barely breathe as Emily took a step towards the tub. I wanted to pull her back. I wanted to run. When she pulled the curtain, my heart dropped into the pit of my stomach. Chance McAvoy stood there, wearing nothing but a smirk: beside him, an equally naked Aiden. I lunged. I don't know at whom, I just lunged. "You son of a bitch. Mother fucker."

Em blocked me. "Cody!"

"Get out of my way Em."

"Noooo." She said calming, but I lunged again. "No! Cody. We have to get out of here. Right now. There's cops here, remember? We could get suspended."

I slammed my hand on the wall and pointed at Aiden. "You stay the fuck away from me."

"Beaumont. I'm sorry."

"Fuck you. The only thing you're sorry about is that you got caught." I shook my head. "All that shit about having a girlfriend and being straight and I find you with him." I laugh and point at Chance. "With HIM! Seriously?" I grabbed Emily's hand and dragged her with me; ignoring Aiden's pleas.

I shivered against the cold as we made our way to Emily's car.

Drawn on the window in the dew was Ashton's name inside of a heart. This was just my luck.

CHAPTER SEVEN

Confrontation

Em and I sat in her car for a good half hour. We talked about boys, mostly about Aiden and how he was a giant douche, how Chance was a freakin' slut and how Ashton did indeed have a huge cock. "I swear to God, I was not expecting it to be so…"

"Big?" Emily smiled that 'I-told-you-so smile.'

"Well, yeah. It was big…. but it was beautiful too."

Emily giggled like a little girl.

"What?"

"I've seen my share of cocks, I have yet to see one that was beautiful." Emily looked at me. "What makes a dick beautiful."

"It's an eye of the beholder thing. But, Em, I swear, it was perfection. Of course… Aiden has a beautiful dick too. Maybe I'm just dick crazy

"Maybe." Emily agreed. "Aiden is a fucking Adonis. It makes sense that his dick would be beautiful.

I banged my head on the headrest. "I should have just said no."

"The day you or *anybody* says no to Aiden Pike… I'll be farting butterflies."

I barked a laugh. "Oh Em, you do paint a picture." It was true though. No one said no to Aiden Pike; at least no one in his or her right mind.

Emily's phone beeped. "Shit. It's my dad. I gotta go. I looked at the digital clock in the dashboard. It was 2:30 in the morning. I leaned over and hugged her.

"Thanks for setting me up. If I'd have known …"

"You told me to never set you up again." She complained.

It was true. She had set me up with a string of losers; all of them after one thing. Ashton as it turns out, wasn't any different than the rest, except that maybe, just maybe I was. "Fine. The embargo is lifted."

I hugged her again and got out of the car. I waited as she started the car and watched her taillights disappear around the corner.

"Beaumont." I jumped at his voice.

"What the fuck are you doing here?" I took a step back as he emerged from the shadows.

"I wanted to explain."

"Explain? Explain what?" I don't know why I was suddenly so angry. Jealousy, maybe. "Did you fuck him?"

"No!"

"Were you going to?"

"No. I mean... I wasn't planning on it. We just..."

"You're a fucking asshole." I rolled my eyes and headed for the front door.

"I wanted it to be with you!" He shouted in frustration.

I pivoted mid stride and went straight up to him, pounding his chest with my palms. "Oh really? It didn't look like you minded so much who it was with." Aiden had the decency to blush. "As a matter of fact, you looked like you were enjoying yourself." I gave him another shove. He grappled for my arms but I shrugged him off and he stumbled backwards. "You need to go. Now."

"No. Not until you let me explain."

"Okay! Explain!"

"Shit, Beaumont. I don't know." Aiden jammed his hands in his coat pockets.

"Go home Aiden." I sighed and turned back towards the front door.

"I've never had a gay friend." His voice was soft and pleading.

"What's that supposed to mean? I'm supposed to be your friend, not your *gay* friend. Why does that make a difference?"

"You know it does."

"No..."

"Yes it does." He was adamant. "You can't tell me that if I was gay, our friendship would be the same. You like me. *Liked* me." He was kicking at the grass. "I've had plenty of girls like me. I know what to do. What to think. How to feel. Then you came along..."

"Aiden, you knew I was gay." It was my turn to blush. "I mean, come on. Look at you. What did you expect?"

"I expected you to like me." He was staring at his shoes.

"What?"

"I wanted you to like me." He brushed fingers through his hair. "I just didn't expect I'd like you back."

"Huh?" *Did he just say he liked me?* "You like me?"

"Not in a gay way."

I couldn't help but laugh. "Seriously. Did you just say that? In what way exactly?"

"I don't know. I just...that first time we kissed, I was expecting it to be like, I dunno, kissing my brother or something."

"Charming." I was still mad, but I couldn't help but smile.

"I'm serious. What's it like when you kiss a girl?"

I cringed. I remembered the first kiss I had with a girl. I don't even remember her name any more. That alone should tell you something. But it was like kissing a jar of mayonnaise.

Apparently Aiden made note of my reaction. "Exactly. *That's* what I was expecting."

I shook my head. "You stripped completely naked. And then proceeded to take my clothes off. Your dick was rock hard."

"I didn't know what I was doing." He looked up at me, all puppy dog eyes.

"Bullshit."

"What? I just figured..."

"You just figured what? Gay guys kiss naked?"

"I just wanted it to be good for you. You can't tell me it wasn't hot." His smile was back and I felt my resolve weakening."

"You're an egotistical jerk."

"I know."

"You're an ass."

"I know."

"You're a stupid, smug, cocky asshole."

Aiden just nodded. "So, are you gonna forgive me?"

"I shouldn't. I should just turn around and forget you ever existed." Not that that was ever going to happen.

Aiden took a tentative step towards me. Then another. "So we're friends again?"

"Yeah. I guess so." I relented.

"And you're still in love with me."

"Ye...what? No. I'm not in love with you!"

"Okay. I was just checking." He nudged me with his shoulder.

"For the record you're a way better kisser than..."

21

I held up a hand. "Stop! Don't even finish that sentence."

"What. I'm just sayin'."

"Well don't."

"Fine." He grabbed me by my jacket and pulled me into a kiss. It was very cliché.

"You can't just keep doing tha…"

He kissed me again.

CHAPTER EIGHT

Temptation

"Can I stay?"   Aiden was still a little drunk as was I.

"Aiden. I don't think that's a good idea."   He was nudging me towards the front door. "At all."

"Come on. I'll be good."   He crossed a finger over his heart. "I promise."

Oh I have no doubt about that.

"Look I've got my halo."   Aiden pretended to reach into his pocket and pulled out nothing but made a circle with both forefingers and thumbs and raised it over his head. I shook my head as I remembered those hands sent tremors through me. "I'll be the perfect angel."   His cherubic smile battered at my resolve. I didn't remember him to be this charming.

I was still mad, damn it. I wanted to be mad.

Aiden sighed, melodrama in high gear. "Fine. Fine. I'll just walk back over to Chloe's. Get in my car, that's if it hasn't been towed and drive drunk all the way home. I could be killed any number of ways.   Struck by a motorist. Drive into a ditch.   I wouldn't want to put you through the guilt."   He had his hands to his heart, the concern in his voice betrayed by the silly smile on his face.

"Okay. You can stay. But you're sleeping on the floor." I insisted.

He nodded readily. "Sure. Sure."   He gathered me up on his way to the door, rushing us both inside before I changed my mind. He shed his jacket. His t-shirt stretched across his broad chest and shoulders. I forced myself to look away. *What have I done?*

I watched his hustle up the stairs to my room; his ass tucked snuggly in a pair of jeans grabbing my attention.

"I'm gonna take a shower."

Part of me thrilled at the notion that he felt so comfortable with me. There had never been any of that 'he's gay, I'm straight' awkwardness from him. No innuendo, *from him anyways.* I trudged up the stairs, my footsteps heavy as I heard the shhhhh of the shower. I stopped at the bathroom door, my hand resting on the doorknob, my forehead against the door.

Aiden yanked open the door. " I need a tow…" The jeans he wore so perfectly lay puddled on the floor along with a pair of neon green briefs. He used his t-shirt to cover himself.

I was utterly mortified. I looked left and right in quick succession, my mouth working; like a fish out of water, no words coming. There was not a rock big enough I could crawl under. I turned sharply and went into my room and closed the door. "Oh my god. Oh my god. Oh my god."

There was a quiet tap-tap-tap on my door. "Beaumont? I still need a towel."

It was an evil plot. No good deed goes unpunished. I opened the door slowly and peeked out. Aiden had climbed back into his jeans and stood there expectantly. "Just tell me where, I can get it."

I pulled the door all the way open and went to the linen closet. I handed him one of the thick oversized towels. My mind had already conjured an image of him draped in only a towel. Sure I'd already seen him naked, but a towel has it's own connotations.

"What?" He smiled mischievously. "You're picturing me in a towel, aren't you?"

I opened my mouth to reply.

He took my hand. "Come on."

I followed, my internal dialogue a cacophonous litany of swear words and doomsday warnings to which I turned a deaf ear. I was shaking my head. He closed the door quietly behind us, sealing my fate. The steamy mirrors showed nothing of my anxiety

"We can't." My voice was barely above a whisper.

"Okay." He pulled at my t-shirt, lifting it up and over my head. He kissed the base of my neck.

"You're supposed to be good." I whined.

He leaned against me licking the base of my neck. I shuddered as his hands worked at my jeans. "I'll be good tomorrow."

The expression, weak in the knees, that cliché romance novel experience of the besotted damsel...maybe it was the heat and steam from the shower, maybe it was the remnants of the alcohol, or maybe it was Aiden working his lips down my neck to my chest to my abs; whatever it was, my knees gave out. I nearly fell, but Aiden grabbed me, holding me up. I draped my arms over his shoulders for support. He smiled up at me and every ounce of determination fled. I kissed him. Not one of those quick innocent pecks, no I flung my whole self into that kiss, knocking us both to the floor. He laughed into the kiss and I kissed him more. I was hungry for him.

I pushed away from him. This was not supposed to be happening. I knew me. And even more importantly, I knew him. "Aiden stop. We can't."

"What?" He looked lost.

"We can't do this." My breathing was heavy, my words forced.

"Damn it Beaumont." He grabbed my hands and pulled me up and towards the shower. "Just tonight. Just you. Just me. Everything else doesn't matter."

It sounded like a line. If it weren't for the earnestness in his eyes the sincerity in his voice, I would have laughed. We stepped under the spray of hot water and my conflict washed away.

I don't remember the shower, not much of it. I remember his hands on me, I remember his lips on me, I remember the water cascading off of him. I remember him pressed against me, pressed inside of me, his gentle words as he thrust inside, me pressed against the cold tile. I remember his throaty moans and me lifted on my toes and lastly, I remember him whispering my name over and over and over as he climaxed, his face buried in the crook of my neck muttering words I'm certain I was not supposed to hear.

"I love you, Cody."

CHAPTER NINE

I Heard It from a Friend

"What are you doing?" Aiden pulled me tighter against him, wrapping his arms around my chest, his lips just behind my ear.

"Nothing." I guess he could feel my smile.

"No, just now, what were you doing?"

This time I laughed. "Do you have a cat?" I burrowed my face in the pillow, still laughing.

"Noooooo…"

"Okay." I tried to pull a straight face "Then this is gonna sound stupid. "I…I was purring." I laughed again. I couldn't help myself. I tried covering my face, certain I was blushing.

"Purring?" He turned me until I was lying on my back. One of his legs was under me, while the other he draped across my thighs. "That has to be the cutest thing I have ever…"

I rolled my head on the pillow to look at him. "You ever tell anyone, and I'll end you."

It was his turn to laugh. "Oh okay, tough guy." He feigned panic, until I reached down between us and grabbed him. "I know your kryptonite." He thrust against my grip.

"That's not kryptonite." He grabbed both my hands and pushed them above my head as he climbed on top of me. He leaned in and stole a kiss. I lifted my head trying to keep contact but he pulled away. Then he dove in for another, plucking kisses like flowers. I was pinned firmly.

"Not fair." I whined

We were both suddenly hard, him thrusting slowly between my legs. I arched my back and wrapped my legs around his waist as he stabbed at me, teasing me. He gained entrance, thrusting in deep. He let my hands go, wrapping his arms under mine, holding me in place as he thrust in again and again. I clawed at his back and bit his shoulder to keep from yelling. I wrapped my legs tighter around him. I tried pushing back against his thrusts, wanting him deeper inside of me. Each thrust was more fervent. He threaded an arm under and around my waist, the other arm he planted against the mattress and pushed.. Before I knew it, we were upright and I was impaled on him, him leaning back on one taut muscled arm, thrusting deep into me, and hitting that mysterious spot. I lost all control and came. "Oh shit. Oh shit. Oh shit." The friction of his abs against my cock was an exquisite torture. I tried to pull away, but he held me firm with one arm, thrusting harder and harder until he quickly pulled out, sending a stream of cum splashing across my chest. His head was thrown back, eyes pinched closed, every muscle was taut and his roar filled the room. He collapsed atop me, gasping for breath. I wrapped my arms around him. I didn't want to let go, I couldn't.

His phone rang. He groaned against my neck. He tried to get up but I held fast. "Don't answer." The light green glow of his phone against the wall winked out. I sighed against his chest. I burrowed against him, soaking up his body heat.

His phone rang again.

"Shit."

"Aiden don't."

He disentangled himself and reached over to the nightstand. Grabbing his phone, I saw him grimace. "Shit." He climbed out of bed, his back to me.

"Hey." Aiden whispered.

I could hear Sophie, her voice shrill.

"Babe. Don't worry. I…I know. I know I was supposed to call you. I'm sorry…Babe. Listen. Sophie…Sophie…Would you let me talk! Listen. I locked my keys in the car. That's all. No…I got a ride home for the spare and then I hung out with a friend…No…No. That's all. I swear. Sophe. You know I love you…What…What? With who? Sophe, come on. Really? You think I would…so why would you believe something like that?..."

I crawled out of bed and went to the window. I grabbed my pack of Marlboros and lighter and climbed out. I could see my breath. I closed the window, hoping I wouldn't hear anymore of Aiden's conversation. Shadows stretched across my yard under the streetlights and I saw a cat's yellow eyes peering up at me.

When I lit my cigarette, it skittered away. I could hear it running through the dry leaves. I pulled my blanket up against the cold.

I heard Aiden open the window. I could smell our sex. I took a long pull on the cigarette and stared out at nothing.

"Cody." He reached for my shoulder but I jerked away from his touch. "Cody."

"Don't…Don't call me that."

"What?"

"You've known me for a fucking month, over a month and have never called me that. It's always been Beaumont. Until last night."

"Look Co…"

"I said, don't fucking call me that!" Somewhere I heard a dog barking. "I could hear her." I glanced back at him and got the satisfaction of seeing him blanche. "Sophie. I could hear what she saying. That you were with *that fag Cody Beaumont*." I wiped at my eyes with my shoulder, my teeth starting to chatter.

"Co…" Aiden started.

"God Damn it! Shut the fuck up. Look. You got what you wanted." I struggled with my lighter to relight my cigarette; my hands were shaking.

"Now you know." Aiden stared at me blankly. "What all the fuss is about."

"Come inside. It's too cold out here. Come back to bed."

My laugh was angry. "Do me a favor, *Pike.* Get the fuck out of my house. Get the fuck out of my life. Just go the fuck away."

"Beaumont."

"I'm serious. I don't want to know you. If I could forget…" I took a long drag on my cigarette and stared at the streetlight. I could see moths flitting in and around the halo of yellow light.

I heard him getting dressing. I saw the swatch of bright light as he came out the front door. I watched him walk away, hearing his footsteps diminish in the night. Then I let myself cry.

CHAPTER TEN

Cold As Ice

"Okay. Get up." Em stood at my bedroom door, her hands on her hips.

I pulled the blankets and sheets over me and burrowed into the warmth of my bed.

"I mean it Cody. You know me. I don't throw parties. Especially pity parties."

I knew what was coming next so I wrapped my arms around my blanket holding on as tight as I could.

"Now. Get. Up!" With each word she tugged on my blankets. I felt myself sliding towards the foot of the bed. Emily was strong. I mean freakishly strong. I attribute that to growing up with four brother. To hear her tell it, they were a family of five brothers.

"Emmmmmmm!" I let go of the blanket in surrender and watched her stumble back.

"Don't Em me. You've been in that bed..." She waved a hand and then pulled the collar of her t-shirt up over her nose, scrunching her face. "... For way too long. I think you're starting to spoil." She coughed for dramatic affect.

"It's not that bad." I sniffed my arm pits.

"You remember that time we went to the zoo..." She made gagging sounds. We were walking through the Chimpanzorium and two chimps going at it, having sex and at the same time, one of them was answering the other call to nature.

I rolled my eyes and sat up. "It doesn't smell like monkey shit in here."

"No. It smells like someone shoved a ripe banana up your..."

"Oh that's cute."

"I'm just saying it smells like..."

"Fine. Fine." I pulled the sheet up to my chest and looked at Emily. "Do you mind?"

"Oh please. You think with four brothers I haven't seen what you're hiding under there. I know you Cody Beaumont. I'm not leaving till you're out of bed."

"Fine." I flung the sheet off of me dramatically. I was stark naked underneath. There! You happy. You've turned me into an exhibitionist." I stood up brazenly and gave her a quick peck on the nose as I strode past on my way to the bathroom.

Oh and Cody."

I turned around winning my struggle not to cover up with my hands. "Yeah." I said with all the nonchalance I could muster.

"Be sure to brush your teeth."

While I shot deadly daggers at her, she whipped out her phone and dropped down on my giant beanbag, I had half a mind to tell her we Aiden and I had sex on that bean bag just two days ago. Instead I slunk off to the bathrrom for my shower.

~~~~~~~

"I can't believe you've never been here." Emily shoved another spoonful of ice cream in her mouth."

I looked around. The place was packed with kids from high school, a few heads bent over books and homework, but the majority of the activity was at the back of the restaurant where a herd of jocks and cheerleaders were holding court. Sporadic laughter, like gunfire echoed up to the front. No one seemed to notice. "It's too."

"Stop. Don't be hating on the Toad." She pointed her plastic red spoon at me like a sword.

"I thought you were on a diet." It was like time came to an abrupt stop.

"You, Cody Beaumont, are a complete ass."

"I didn't mean. I... Em..." I fumbled

"No you're right. Fat old Emmy needs to stay away from the ice cream."

"Em, you're not even fat. You're perfect." I leaned over the table and whispered. "If I weren't gay, I'd so have monkey sex with you."

"That's sweet." She pretended to flick hair out of her face. "But I have standards."

I threw my maraschino cherry at her. She caught it deftly, plopping it in her mouth. I stirred the remnants of my ice cream.

"Okay. Spill it. The pity party ban is lifted. Just this once."

I shook my head.

"I can have him taken out. Seriously. Four brothers. Just say the word."

I smiled halfheartedly. "I just need to forget all about him."

"A distraction.. Emily put a hand to her chin. "Hmmmm. I know just the thing."

"Em." I closed my eyes.

"Oh look who it is."

I knew who it was before I opened my eyes. I could almost taste the cloves.

"Hi Ems." Ashton's voice was a little hesitant. "What are you *doing* here?" His jaw tightened. I knew instantly that like myself, Ashton wasn't apart of this impromptu plan of hers.

I looked at him. His name was embroidered in white stitching across an orange sherbet colored apron. He was carrying a bus tub filled with dirty glasses and if looks could kill, Emily would be engulfed in a pillar of flames.

I couldn't help but smile. "Hi Ashton." His cheeks were slightly flushed.

"When's your break?" Em played completely oblivious to his embarrassment.

Ashton looked over his shoulder at a giant frog shaped clock on the wall behind the counter. "'Bout ten minutes."

"Good." She scooted over to the window and patted the spot where she was sitting.

Ashton rolled his eyes and twirled around giving me an adorable smile as he did. "Fine. See you in ten." I tried not to watch him walk away, but with the apron tightly cinched around his waist and those skinny jeans, I couldn't help myself.

Emily looked at me, her smile blooming hugely. "See. I helped." She bounced in her seat. She looked over my shoulder as laughter filled the back of the restaurant. Her smile faltered. "Don't look around. Whatever you do."

I hate those words. I sat perfectly still breathing as little as possible.

"Shit." Emily looked down, running hand through the back of her hair. "I'm sorry Cody."

Aiden and Sophie walked past. I could smell his cologne. Sophie whispered into his ear then grabbed his arm and laughed into the shoulder of his letter jacket; her glance back at me, pure contempt. Aiden didn't acknowledge my existence, just walked stiffly, staring straight ahead.

CHAPTER ELEVEN

Broken hearts

"Wow. The queen bitch just shot you a look." Ashton plopped down next to Emily. "She find out about you and whatshisface?"

Emily broke the awkward silence that followed. "We're not talking about that."

"Oh, okay." He squeezed ketchup all over his fries. The bottle made a squirting sound and he closed the lid and pounded it on the table. "Damn Trish didn't fill up her bottles." He got up and stole the ketchup from the table behind us, hefting it to make sure it wasn't empty first.

So you work here?" I know. I know. I'm lame. The last time I saw him, I had his dick in my mouth.

Ashton looked up at me, his face quizzical. "No. No. I just stole this apron and had my name embroidered on it."

Emily sneezed and I looked at her as she shook from suppressed laughter. I kicked her under the table. "Bitch."

Ashton laughed. "Yeah. I work here. " He nudged Emily with his shoulder. "She'd still work here too if she wasn't such a ho bag."

"What?" This was news to me.

"Oh yeah. It was during the summer. They hired like 6 of us, right before school started, for after the football games." He stuck a couple of fries in his mouth and chewed fast. "It gets crazy busy after football games. Tips are awesome." Aston grabbed his burger and took a huge bite.

Emily was surprisingly quiet. I wondered why she hadn't told me she had worked here, apparently ever so briefly. Then it occurred to me that it was about the same time that Aiden and I started hanging out.

33

"Anyway, I think it was me and Ems and..." he paused to think. "...And Katie I think. Katie's worked here longer. Anyway, Ems and Katie were flirting with these guys. It was dead in here. Nobody but us three and three baseball players, still in their uniforms after practice. I was in heeeeeeaven." He pretended to fan himself with his hand as he drank his soda. "They were gorgeous. Straight as flagpoles, but gorgeous." He leaned over the table in my direction. His eyes were sparkling and mischievous. "I was too....straight as a flagpole." He sat back and sucked on his straw seductively. I felt his shoe nudge mine. "Anyway before you know it, you have these three gorgeous baseball players gobbling down sundaes. It was hottie Ems hottie Katie hottie." He pointed to an imaginary lineup of people.

"I love it how the baseball players get called hottie while us girls are just named." Emily smacked Ashton in the shoulder. I felt a momentary twinge of jealousy. Emily was *my* friend.

"Hey, if I knew their names, I wouldn't be here right now. I'd probably be Mr. Baseball player number 3." He sighed. "Anyway. Long story short, Ems here, decided that they didn't have to pay for the sundaes if she could get their numbers"

I pretended to be scandalized. "You harlot. Jezebel. Slut!" I pointed accusingly.

Ashton laughed so hard I think soda came out of his nose He quickly covered his face with a napkin. "That's so gross." He wiped at his face a little more with the napkin. "Anyway. Mr Tweedy."

Both Emily and Ashton leaned against each other. "Tony." They said in unison and broke up in laughter again.

"Mr Tweedy is one of those grown ups, who's your friend, your buddy, your pal." Ashton explained. "He's got one of those pencil thin molester moustaches." He shivered. "Any time he congratulated me he'd put his hand on my shoulder and my skin would just crawl." Ashton's shoulder dipped as if he suddenly felt the hand. "Anyway, Mr. Tweedy fired her on the spot. Wouldn't even listen to Katie tell him it was her idea."

"I miss Katie." Emily looked wistful.

"She works tonight. You could probably even come back to work, now that Tweedy is gone. Katie'd put in a good word. So would I. Three Musketeers together again!"

Katie turned in her seat. "What happened to Tweedy?"

"Oh he got fired. One day he was here, next day we had Rachel. You'd love Rachel. She's awesome."

I stared at Ashton. He was a great deal more animated than our last meeting. His smile drew my eyes. He talked a lot with his hands, quick gestured with those long pale fingers. He scraped the last two French fries across his plate sopping up the last of the ketchup and shoved them in his mouth. He covered his mouth as he spoke. "Come out and smoke with me." He was looking straight at me his eyes asking just as much as his words.

I looked at Emily. She was smiling that 'who's the best Emily in the world' smile. I quirked a smile as she gestured with her head to follow Ashton who had grabbed up his mess and crammed it all in a cubbyhole behind the servers station. He reached further back into another cubbyhole and pulled out a pack of cigarettes and his lighter. I followed him through the back of the restaurant through an EMPLOYEES ONLY door and to a backdoor that had been propped open with a giant jar of pickles.

"Shit." He wadded the empty pack of cigarettes holding the last one.

"Here. You can have one of mine. You can save that one for when you get off." I knocked a few cigarettes from my pack and he took one. He tucked his behind his ear. I could smell the rich clove aroma that I had come to associate with Ashton.

"So…" He lite his cigarette and took a long pull. "I know you have a thing for this Aiden guy. But I was wondering if you'd like to go out…with me…on a date. There's this retro band, they do all these covers of 70s and 80s rock ballads and they're gonna be at Wildfire on Friday."

I leaned back against the brick exterior and grinned over at him. "70s and 80s rock ballads?"

"Hey! That's all I listened to growing up. My dad had his stereo going 24/7, you know cassette tapes and 8 tracks. I mean he grew up with the stuff…" He paused and took another drag off his cigarette. "We can come here before and eat. On me."

"Oh big spender."

We both laughed. "Nothing's to good for my…"

"Sure."

"What?"

"I'll go. With you."

Ashton shook his head, looking down at his shoes, grinning.

"What?"

35

"I dunno. I just have this feeling you're gonna show up in bell bottoms and a bandanna or something."

I choked on my cigarette. "I wouldn't be caught dead in bell bottoms. When I was growing up, like in elementary school, my mom bought these lime green belt bottoms. I think I was traumatized. Even in elementary school. It set back my fashion sense by a decade."

We both watched each other. He crushed out his cigarette.

"Want another one?" I offered.

Ashton shook his head and took a tentative step towards me. He hooked a finger in one of my belt loops and pulled himself against me. "Just so you know. I'm not gonna wait for you to decide whether or not you like me. I like you."

"I like…" I began.

Ashton pressed a finger to my lips and shook his head again. "I know this thing with Aiden is intense. If what you two have is real, then tell me. If it's just sex…"

I shook my head opening my mouth to reply.

"No, let me finish. If it's just sex…"

"Ashton…"

Ashton leaned in and kissed me, shutting me up. "Seriously. Let me finish. *If* it's just sex, have it with me." He smiled, our noses still touching. "I like you. And I'm intense. And I fall fast and hard. And right now I'm on my way down. I love public displays of affection. Holding hands. And if the day comes that you read to me in bed, I swear to god I'll find a way to have your babies."

His stare was so intense I couldn't look away. The thing of it was, I didn't want to look away. I didn't want to go anywhere or do anything. Just stand here; our bodies pressed together, his cute little cold nose pressed against mine, his lips barely brushing mine as he spoke. "One other thing. I know you're going to break my heart."

He shut me up with another kiss before I could even deny such a thing.

You're gonna break my heart." Ashton stated it matter-of-factly. "I know it like I knew it at Chloe's party. When you left me there to chase after Aiden."

I couldn't breathe.

"Honesty scares people. It shouldn't, but it does. Because it's real. You're real." He pressed his hand against my chest and then

36

took mine and pressed it against his chest. "I'm real. So we have to be honest…"

"Where the hell is Ashton?" A woman's voice echoed through the backdoor. She poked her head the doorway.. "Breaks over Romeo." She threw me a glance. "Sorry sport."

Ashton smiled wryly. "That's Rachel. I gotta go." He leaned in, pressing me back against the cold hard brick and kissed me, then tugged me a few steps by my belt loops.

"Damn it!" Ashton signed regretfully and headed back into the restaurant.

"What?" I followed, holding the door as he moved the giant jar of pickles.

"I think I'd quit my job for another kiss. But I got a date on Friday with this guy." He retied his apron, glancing in the full-length mirror to make sure he was presentable. Next to the mirror was a handwritten sign. YOUR SMILE IS PART OF YOUR UNIFORM!

I barked a laugh as he produced a dimpled smile. "God you're fucking adorable."

I tried to keep the smile off my face as I slid back into the booth. Clearly I failed miserably.

"What?"

"That boy is going to be a handful." I held up my hand. "And before you say it, get your mind out of the gutter."

Emily pouted.

She had gotten us refills. The ice had melted in my Dr. Pepper but I drank gratefully.

"Sooooooo?" She looked at me expectantly. "Details. I need details."

"We're going on a date, Friday. Someplace called Wildfire."

"And?"

"And what?"

"Ingrate. And thank you Emily for being the best Emily in the world. You know it's never going to catch on if you don't say it." She shook her head, sighing with exaggeration. "Good sycophants are so hard to find."

"My apologies oh great one." I drank the rest of my Dr. Pepper.

"Better. Still needs a little work. But it'll do. For now." She grabbed her purse and pulled out a little mirror and some lip-gloss.

I watched her for a couple of seconds then said. "He said I'm gonna break his heart."

She snapped the mirror closed and looked over at me. "You're a heartbreaker."

"I'm not a…" Nobody ever let's me finish a sentence.

"Hatatatatatata…." Emily held up her hand. "It's not that you do it on purpose. You're just a good guy."

"What? That doesn't even make sense."

"Think about it. He's afraid he's going to break your heart. And *that* is going to break his heart." Emily crammed the lip-gloss back into her purse.

"Wait. So he's gonna break *my* heart?" I laid my forehead on the table. "I'm confused."

"It's no wonder men are the weaker sex. Even the gay ones are clueless."

I rolled my head on the table so that I could glare at her.

"What? It's true." She reached for my cup but found it empty. "Look. Here it is." She held her hands up dramatically. "Emily's history in a nutshell. Since the beginning of time, through the best of intentions and the worst, man has destroyed everything he's ever put his hands on. Everything. Why would a heart be any different?"

CHAPTER TWELVE

Say Something

I was waiting on Em. She had my history book and my notes for the trig test in fifth period. I watched for her car. It was hard to miss; ugly burnt orange VW Beetle in need of a new paint job, a new bumper…a new everything.

"Is it true?"

Really? I couldn't help but laugh. I was a little incredulous that Aiden had the audacity to confront me about anything so my laughter was jaded as I shook my head.

"Is it? Are you and Ashton Prince…?" I could see his words. It looked like we were smoking; the air was so cold, his words punctuated with plumes of his frosty breath.

"Aiden. What do you want?" I looked away, hopping from one foot to another, trying to keep warm. Aiden and I were at the top of the steps in front of Fairweather High. The school was built on a hill and from the top of the steps you could see for miles. On clear days, it was beautiful; the whole town lay below, bordered by a silver line that was the river. Today, the wet cold dampened everything in a gray blanket. I pushed my hands into the pockets of my hoodie and stepped down from the top step.

"Beaumont…"

"No!" I looked around; surprised my voice was so loud, surprised at its vehemence. A few faces turned in our direction.

"No." I whispered, stepping back up and getting into his face. "You don't get to ask me questions. You don't get to talk to me. You don't get..." *Me.* I choked on that last word. My words struck him like blows. He wilted under the barrage. "You need to leave me alone."

"Cody..."

"No." I looked at him and shook my head. "No. Don't ask me anything. Don't say anything. There's nothing you can say that's going to change how I feel; like a complete fool, like I should hate you. But I don't want to hate you. I don't want to think about you. I don't want..."

"I did. I did say something. I said *it.*" I watched his teeth chatter, his lips vibrating, his breath a white plume of words pushed by the wind.

I turned away, fighting the memory, but falling into it. I could hear him say it; I could feel him, the intimacy of the moment. It was devastating. I shook my head, fighting tears. I sniffed; telling myself it was just the cold. "Your timing was perfect, you know, with your d..."

"I meant it."

I looked at him, my face a mask of confusion. "That you love me?" Saying it, the words burdened me more than lifted me up. They were supposed to buoy the spirit, those three words: I love you. But they were a sad song, sung over and over in my head. I looked at him stony faced. "And you love Sophie. Don't forget that." I turned again and took the stone steps, two at a time, as fast as I could. I didn't listen, but heard him calling after me. I stumbled a little at the bottom, the gravel tripping me up, but I kept my footing. Then I raced to my car, past unfamiliar faces all looking after me as I ran. At one point I was lost, turning this way and that, looking for my car, my tears as cold and heavy as the gray morning air. I dropped down to my knees, the gravel biting. I wanted to yell at the top of my lungs, bellow out this pain, this hate. A horn blared behind me. I looked back. Em.

She was out of the car, running to me, grabbing me tight and rocking me back and forth, her words a whispered calming mantra. I tried hard not to break down any further, burying my face in the warmth of her embrace, but her words, that moment of unconditional love, her arms around me, protecting me against myself, I cried. Great sobs racked me, battering my soul. Em cried too, holding my face in her hands, wiping my tears with her thumbs while hers own tears flowed freely. "Come on. Let's go. Come on. Get up." She lifted me up, slipping her arms under mine. I felt miniscule, weak. "She walked me to the passenger side of her car, opening the door and letting me slip into the seat. She reached over me and fastened me in, making sure it was tight. Closing the door, she stood outside and I could see she was looking up, up the hill, up those stone steps. I turned my head and I could still see him up there. He was pressed back against the doors, his shoulders hunched against the cold.

Em ran around the front of the car and jumped in. We raced through the parking lot. I could hear the *tit tit tit* of gravel hitting parked cars. She pulled to a sudden stop at the base of the steps.

"Em. Don't. Let's just go." I pleaded.

Emily was out of the car and running up the steps. She ran straight at him. He stood, staring directly at me, as she pummeled his chest. She pushed him, yelling. I could hear her, but not her words. She gestured wildly. He towered over her but she went at him with the ferocity of a warrior. Watching it brought more tears. I grimaced as she brought a quick knee to his groin. His stoic stance faltered and he slumped to his knees, a fallen combatant. I gripped the door handle but didn't have the strength, the will, to open it. I watched as Emily strode down the steps, this time slowly and steadily, her breath following her in plumes. At the top of the steps, on his knees, Aiden collapsed back against the brick wall. I couldn't tell if he was laughing or crying, but plumes of his breath floated above him as if he were afire.

CHAPTER THIRTEEN

Date Night

"No."

"What?" I looked in the mirror pivoting left and right.

"You can't wear that." Seriously Cody. You're going to a club, not Sunday Mass." Emily went into the walk in closet and started tossing clothes out.

"Hey. You're going to clean that up." I picked up my BOTDF t-shirt. "How bout this?"

Emily looked over her shoulder. "Yeah cuz Blood on the Dance Floor is the epitome of 80s cover band. Absolutely not!"

"Fine. Just pick out what you want me to wear. Dress me like a Ken doll." I plopped down on my bed, staring at the ceiling.

"Oh! I've always wanted an anatomically correct Ken doll." Emily laughed.

"Slut!"

"And after I'm finished with you, you're gonna look like one too."

"Oh great."

"Seriously. You'll look great." Emily stood in the doorway to the closet, frustrated. "We really need to go shopping. When's the last time you bought something that didn't have a band name on it or a bird flying across it somewhere."

"What?"

"It's time to go buy some grownup clothes."

I scrunched up my nose. Don't look at me like that. "Yeah, I'm gonna dress you up like Mr. Rogers." She pretended to button up a cardigan. Won't you be my neighbor?" She mimicked.

I laughed. "You know, I read on the Internet that he was a Marine sniper. 42 confirmed kills." I pretended to aim a sniper rifle.

Emily looked dubious through my imaginary scope. "Yeah, I heard he served with Captain Kangaroo and Captain Crunch." She came out of the closet and grabbed her purse off of my dresser. "Come on. We're going shopping. And don't make that face."

"What?" *Did I make a face?*

"Trust me. You're gonna be a babe magnet." Emily reassured.

"Just what every gay man likes to hear."

"Shut up and let's go." Emily pulled me up off the bed and dragged me through the apartment.

I hated the mall. I mean besides walking by the Abercrombie & Fitch store and smelling the cologne wafting from the entrance. I'd heard they sprayed it on the clothes in the morning before opening. I just wanted to wallow in the fragrance. Emily was rather fond of the scent as well. We made it a point to walk by at least 5 or 6 times as we went from shop to shop in search of my new look. She finally broke down and went in and bought a bottle of Fierce. I swear we got high off the stuff. That's the only reason I could fathom her reenactment of the Meg Ryan scene from *When Harry Met Sally.* There we were sitting on one of the benches right next to the food court. I was devouring a pretzel from Auntie Anne's making yummy noises as I chewed. Emily was wrestling with the plastic wrap on her cologne purchase. She looked at me with those puppy dog eyes and while I held the pretzel in my mouth, I ripped the cellophane off. She leaned in, kissed my cheek and took a bite out of my pretzel. I waved her away with slapping gestures. "Mine!" So maybe it was the pretzel, maybe it was the cologne, but the next thing I know, she's having a fake orgasm right next to me. A woman wearing a horrible purple fleece jumpsuit looked scandalized.

"Auntie Anne's. They really do make good pretzels." I held the vestiges of my pretzel up like I was in a commercial, projecting a deep voice. Emily burst out into laughter. She wove her arm through mine, leaning against me. Purple fleece jumpsuit was not impressed.

We ended up getting a pair of khaki's, slim fit, a really cute button down Oxford which "brought out my eyes", a pair of jeans that "made my ass look fabulous" and the cutest pair of underwear I'd ever seen. She nixed the superman briefs. "We're getting big boy clothes." Along with the superman briefs, she rejected every t-shirt with anything printed on it, any pair of shredded jeans I even looked at and a cute beanie with kitty cat ears. I meowed incessantly until She let me get two deep V-necks from Urban Outfitters, (they were on sale) so I forgave her.

We were sitting in the food court for lunch. My Big Mac was utter perfection and Emily got the 20-piece chicken McNuggets. "You know, give me a good electric current and we can build our own Frankenchicken."

Emily threw one of her nuggets at me. I caught it in my mouth, raising my hands and bellowed victoriously. Emily rolled her eyes. "Gross."

"You love me."

"Okay. Haircut."

"Huh? What? I don't want a haircut!" I ran a hand through my hair. I hadn't had it cut for about six months. My bangs were monstrous.

"Too bad! I've already made the appointment. I got Laz to cut it for me."

I raised my eyebrows, impressed. Lazarus Dane was an artist. Seriously. You've seen those commercial on TV for starving artist shows at the big hotels, that's what he did. In between art shows though, he cut and styled hair. He was a little Avant-garde for my taste. The last thing I wanted was something that looked like waterfowl taking off into the air from the top of my head.

His salon was right next to the mall. Emily parked her VW between a late model Mercedes Benz and a gorgeous midnight Blue BMW. Clearly Emily drove the proverbial redheaded stepchild of the German motor industry.

"What are we doing with this?" He ran his fingers through my hair, pulling up my bangs. He bent lower and peered over my head, where all I could see was his eyes.

"Laz, you're scaring him."

"I need to see what he sees. It's all perspective." Laz straightened up and circled the chair twice, taking hold of my chin, pivoting my head at various angles.

I eyed Emily nervously. "I just want a trim."

Lazarus scoffed and grabbed his electric clippers. "Lazarus Dane doesn't do trims.

The final product, I have to say, turned out way better than I had expected. Emily dropped me off, both of us exhausted. I wanted a nap so bad before my date. I couldn't keep from smiling at the idea that I was going on a date. A real date. "You're so cute." Emily smiled and handed me a Hot Topic bag.

"What's this for?" I looked inside. It was the kitty cat beanie. "Meow?" I reached over and hugged her. "You're the best."

"The best...?" She stretched the question as if I'd forgotten something.

"Oh. Oh yeah." I cleared my throat. " The best Emily in the whole world." I said it in a monotone robotic voice.

"That's my pet." She gave my head a little shove. "Now get out."

~~~~

"Wow! You clean up nice."

I had decided on the jeans and the dark gray and white V-neck. I was in front of the mirror so long I started hearing *You're So Vain* in Emily's voice in the back of my head. My haircut was cute as hell, but I messed with it for at least an hour anyway before I gave up, realizing I couldn't make it any better than Lazarus already had.

I blushed. "Thanks. You look amazing." He was wearing a black button down, jeans and a cute pair of gray Frye Harness boots that I coveted almost immediately.

"You don't mind eating here, do you? We can go somewhere else." He leaned into me as we walked through the parking lot. "I just want to show off my date."

"Stop. You're making me swoon." I pretended to fan myself as he held open the door.

The football must not have let out yet as the Frozen Toad was still quiet. A few families sat in booths along the back and the ice cream counter had only two occupants. We walked past the counter, Ashton reaching down and twirling one of the red faux leather bar stools. Our waitress was a girl named Katie.

Ashton looked at me. "D'you know Katie?"

I shook my head.

45

"You'd love her. Her and Ems are like two peas in a pod. I swear, sometimes I hear Katie talking and I look up and it's Ems and visa versa." I smiled, not knowing what to say to that. "So. I heard about…you know." *God, I hope he didn't want to talk about that.* "I just wanted to say…you know…what I said before. Until you tell me otherwise, there's no Aiden Pike. It is what it is, between the two of you." He reached across the table and took my hand. "You and me. That's my priority." He squeezed my hand then let go.

We ate in awkward silence and I was afraid the rest of the evening was shot to hell. Then Katie came and sat down for a minute. "So this is him?" She sized me up while I did a double take. Her voice, the inflection, the hint of sarcasm, it was all Emily. I couldn't help but grin. "Slummin' it?" She asked me.

"Not at all." My voice caught in my throat and I blushed.

"Oh. Ash, he's a keeper."

Ashton grinned mischievously. "Maybe. We'll see. He looks musically illiterate. I can't have that."

I laughed. I'd told him as much the other night when he called. We had talked for two hours about everything; books, (he was an avid reader,) comics (Marvel was definitely better than the DC Universe) Movies, (I'd have to sit through horror movies while he endured the chic flicks that I so adored), favorite "old movie star" (definitely George Clooney) and music.

"I love music." I scrambled to defend myself. "It's just, I don't remember who sings what and what it's called and I don't listen to the radio."

"Tsk Tsk Tsk." I imagined him smiling, maybe laying in his bed like I was, the lights off, the blanket pulled up high against the encroaching cold. "I'll have to fix that."

"Please do."

"….Cody?" Ashton smirked. "Where'd you go?"

"Nowhere." I blinked.

"Okay boys. Have fun." Katie rose determined, nodding in the direction of a raucous group of kids. "I've got a table of devil's spawn back there I have to get back to before they destroy the place."

Ashton gave her a pitying smile then looked over at me. "You ready?"

We took Ashton's car. It was a little dirtier than I expected and I choked at the overpowering scent of clove. "Sorry. I lost track of time or I would have cleaned it."

I shook my head. "'S'okay." I could tell he was embarrassed. "Seriously." I took his hand. It was warm, his long fingers so fine and delicate, but his grip was firm.

The band was so good. I don't know how many times I said the words "I love this song." If you asked me the names, I'd have to plead ignorance, but loved them I did. Ashton and I sang along with a couple of them and his laugh was infectious when I caught him singing boisterously to a song I'd never heard. We danced a couple of times and he sang in my ear, his lips and warm breath sending chills through me. I was terribly pleased with myself when the band sang a song I recognized that Ashton did not. I sang loudly, whatever inclinations I had for introversion, all but forgotten.

"Did you have fun?" Ashton and I sat in his car. He'd cracked the windows so we could smoke. I kept looking at him. He had a sleepy smile, much like the one he'd had the first night I met him.

"You even have to ask?" His fingers were entwined with mine.

Smoke curled from his lips as he asked. "So, you gonna kiss me or what?" I dropped my cigarette through the crack in the window and pulled him to me.

CHAPTER FOURTEEN

Books & Cloves

"Oh my god! Did you hear?"

Ashton had found a Starbucks that was still open and we sat at one of the tiny tables, our knees pressing as he leaned forward, a whip cream moustache making him all the more adorable. I ran my thumb across his upper lip and it took all my willpower not to fling the table aside when he sucked off the whip cream..

You're bad." I pulled my hand from his grasp. "And heard what?"

"Chance McAvoy."

"I couldn't really care less." I had no desire whatsoever to listen to any of the extra curricular activities of Chance McAvoy, especially after everything that happened.

Ashton wilted at my response.

"Okay. Fine. What about Chance McAvoy."

"He's a twin!"

I looked at Ashton liked the heavens opened up, all the questions of the universe were suddenly made clear and I had just won the lottery, and then dropped the façade, quirking an eyebrow. "Yeah, so…"

"So, apparently, no one knew he had a twin. And I mean no one and they've both been pretending to be Chance. Same clothes, same haircut, same everything… Get this. Their father, is like this huge business mogul, is never home, and they've been doing this ever since they moved to Fairweather. I mean. I knew him or… I guess them…in high school."

"Well that explains it."

"Explains what?"

"How he could be such a hoe bag."

Ashton scowled. "Do you even know Chance?"

"By reputation. And you saw him at Chloe's party." I drank my frap, looking out the window, watching the late night traffic zip past on the highway. "Look. Can we just talk about something else?"

"Yeah" He nodded quickly, taking a quick drink. "Yeah. How 'boouut…we talk about your singing skills."

"What are you saying?" I grinned. "I told you: musically illiterate." I tapped my chest.

"I'm thinking YouTube sensation." He made marquee hand gestures, looking up wide-eyed and adorable.

"Oh please, you're full of shit." I sat back, chewing on my straw, watching his eyes sparkling."

"I dunno. I was swooning big time. Couldn't take my eyes off of you."

"Me? What about you? It was like I was at an Ashton Prince concert. I only knew the words to like maybe two, three songs max. You knew almost all of 'em."

"Yeah, what was that one song you sang? Oh my god you were so perfect."

I felt silly, grinning and blushing while he looked at me like that. I shook my head and looked down at my hands.

"What?"

I took a deep breath. "I was just wondering how I was going to convince you to take me home." I bit my lip. This wasn't my first date, not for a long time, but it felt like it.

"Oh yeah?" He smiled so big; his eyes were almost completely closed.

I nodded. We sat there for a moment, just looking across the table at one another. Then he grabbed his keys, his phone, and my hand in quick succession and we ran for the door laughing. He pressed me against the passenger side of the car and kissed me. "Mine or yours?" He asked breathlessly after breaking our kiss. "Mine's closer."

I was almost willing to have sex right there in the Starbucks parking lot. "Yours. Yours. Yours." I chanted.

"So, mine then?"

I unclasped his belt and slid a hand in past his waste band. "It's either yours or here." I gave him a quick squeeze. He growled, his face buried in my neck. He gave it a quick bite before pushing off against the car and running around to the other side. . "Get in!"

I don't want to say he raced home, but I was forced on several turns to steady myself on the dashboard or grip the armrest.

He lived in a new development on the north side of Fairweather. I loved the apartments. I had looked at them, on a whim, but they were way out of my price range. "You live here?"

He jingled his keys then opened the door. "Come on." He waited at the door and placed a hand on my waist as we climbed the stairs to his place. "It's up to the left."

The apartment was nothing like I was expecting. The light was muted, the furniture dark classic art deco, the flooring a slate finished wood. Our footsteps echoed through the apartment as I followed him to the kitchen. He pulled open the refrigerator, the light glancing off chrome surface. He pulled out a bottle of pinot noire and grabbed two glasses by the stems. "Come on." I followed him out onto the balcony. He sat and pulled another chair close to him and patted the patterned cushion. He lit two cigarettes at once and offered me one. I didn't normally smoke clove cigarettes, but I didn't normally drink wine either. I watched him pour.

"You're an enigma."

Ashton looked at me, eyebrows lifted, asking the question that went unspoken.

"I mean, you're a waiter at…what's it called…the Frozen Toad, you live here," I gestured with my hands. "The first time I met you, I thought, emo party boy. That flask in your pocket, " I took a long drag on my cigarette. "Clove cigarettes. Oh and let's not forget, an 80s rock ballad aficionado."

"And you went out with me anyway." He had an ironic tone.

"Well, you're a damn good kissers." I laughed.

"Oh really?" He softly bit the rim of his wine glass as he looked at me. "You're not so bad yourself."

I grinned, feeling the wine.

"What?"

"Em told me you said, and I quote…" I did the rabbit ears, holding my wine glass precariously. "The best kisser."

He laughed blushing and hiding his smile behind a hand. "She told you?"

I pulled his hand down, leaning in and pulling him closer to me and whispered. "Yeah. She ratted to you out."

The kiss was soft. Tentative. Tasting of wine and clove. He twined his fingers with mine. One kiss led to another and then another building in intensity like the kiss in the Starbuck's parking lot, feral and urgent. We both stood, my chair falling back behind me, clattering loudly. He pulled me with him as he walked backward into the apartment, our wine forgotten. We tugged at each other's clothes, all the while kissing fervently. I heard the fabric tear as he pulled at my shirt. I yanked open his shirt, buttons skittering across the wooden floor. He hadn't re-clasped his belt and the buckled jangled as I forced his jeans down. He kicked them off and pushed me backwards onto the bed. He climbed on top of me, straddling my hips, in just his underwear. He looked down at me and I was astonished. Moonlight made him ethereal and I reached up and touched him, traced fingers along the subtle lines of his abs and pecs and then down to the waistband of a pair of bright pink aussieBum undies. "Seriously, those are gonna have to come off."

CHAPTER FIFTEEN

Le Petit Mort

"You slut!" Emily laughed, hand to her mouth, but leaning forward, greedy for the details.

Truth be told, I really wasn't the first date, wham, bam, thank you Sam kind of guy. I liked romance. I liked courtship. I wasn't above receiving a few flowers for Valentine's Day.

"Wait a minute. Like you've never had sex on the first date. And technically, we nearly did it at Chloe's." I paused, certain that wasn't really making my point. I tried a different approach. "Besides, You remember that one guy you did behind the Frozen Toad? What was his name again?" I paused for affect. "Oh that's right, you never got it!"

Emily waved her hands in surrender, unable to talk, her laughter leaving her breathless. It was a good thing she was sitting down. Still she was turning a dangerous shade of crimson. I leaned back, hugging the sofa cushion, feeling smug satisfaction. I grabbed up the funny pages, from the Sunday paper, once again mourning the absence of *Calvin & Hobbes*, while I waited for her to catch her breath.. I settled on *Get Fuzzy*, laughing to myself at Bucky and Satchel's shenanigans. I flipped the top of the paper down and peered over at her. Her laughter had subsided to a few staccato outburst as she wiped tears from her eyes. "In my defense, he left a really big tip."

"Oh well that makes it *all* better."

"Hey! We're not here to talk about me." Emily grabbed her coffee, taking a sip, she watched me over the rim. "Tell me. Everything. Don't leave anything out. Start from the beginning."

"Well, dinner was dinner, nothing glamorous about that. I saw your friend Katie. I swear to God I thought it was you at first. You sound just alike."

Emily inched forward. "I know, right! Almost freaks *me* out. But that's not important. Get to the good stuff."

I glared at her, feigning outrage. "The good stuff? I feel so dirty."

"Oh shut up. Now come on. Emmy needs to live vicariously."

I barked a laugh. "Emmy needs to get laid."

"Well this is the next best thing. Now spill!"

"Fine. Fine. After dinner, we went to Wildfire. Not what I was expecting at all. I don't know why I was expecting a country western theme. I mean, Ashton certainly isn't country and he told me about the band that was gonna be there, but still. Anyway…the band was awesome. Ashton was so cute. He sang like every song and…"

Emily started rolling her hand in that 'hurry up and get to the good stuff' way. "Yeah Yeah Yeah…I know I told you to start from the beginning but I could tell you were about to get all cloyingly sappy about him singing blah blah….blah blah bla blah….blah blah blah… blahblahblahblah! "Pretend you just told me everything right up to the moment where he kisses you and I'll give you all the expected platitudes…oh that's so cute…..how sweet….nuh uh!" Emily set her coffee cup down and folded her knees under her and grabbed one of the plush throw pillows, hugging it in front of her. "Now, the good stuff for fuck's sake."

"So what you really meant, when you said 'Tell me everything. Don't leave anything out, Start from the beginning.' was, tell you the pervy stuff." Emily nodded her head vigorously. "Charming." I took a deep breath, just wondering how to start. "Seriously though." I looked her straight in the eyes. "Have you ever been seduced with just one touch?"

I watched her collapse back onto the plush arm of the sofa, her arms flung backwards over her head, the throw pillow dropping to the floor as she sighed at the notion.

"Seriously, those are gonna have to come off."

Ashton leaned down, his hips undulating over my crotch, teasing me. "I have an idea." He whispered in my ear, his tongue softly lapping at my lobe. "Why don't you take them off." One of my hands was at the small of his back, pulling him tighter against me, but he reached back and slid it further down, under the waistband of his underwear until my fingers lay in the crack of his ass. He pushed my fingers, teasing his tight wet hole with slow intermittent thrusts, arching his back as my finger delved into his warmth. He looked down at me, biting his lip, his hair hanging down, tickling my cheek, his eyes intent on me. I marveled up at him, as he ground ever so softly, barely brushing against my cock that was hard and pressing against the fabric of my underwear. I thrust up to meet him simultaneously slamming him down on top of me, pulling with my hand, a finger buried inside of him. He buried his face in the nook of my neck and shoulder and bit me, the pain exquisite. I arched my back and he slipped an arm under me, flipping us, maneuvering me on top of him.

I looked down at him, watching him breathe, his lips, a red blossom, parted and glistening in the moonlight. He reached up with a delicate hand and traced my lips. I suckled his fingers, then kissed his palm, biting at it. His other hand found it's way to my cock. He massaged me through the fabric and I shuddered at the contact. He grabbed my thighs with both hands and guided me atop his chest. He buried his face in my crotch, his hands kneading my ass. I shook as he grazed his teeth inside my thigh, mouthed my cock through the fabric and then he hooked fingers under the waistband and pulled frantically, releasing me. He kissed the swollen head, running his tongue across the slit before kissing it again.

"What are you doing to me?" I didn't realize I spoke until he smiled up at me.

"Everything." He ran his tongue, slowly, seductively, up the shaft of my cock, not losing eye contact.

The sheets were bunched in my hands, my arms taut as I leaned back on them and thrust softly. He wrapped his lips around me then and all I could do was breathe deeply and chant "oh god oh god oh god oh god." I tried to pull away but he held me firmly as he worked his tongue and mouth. My guttural cry filled the room as I came. I collapsed sideways onto the pillows that had been knocked aside. I couldn't breathe deep enough and panted. "Not fair."

His grin was sly. But two could play at this game. I pawed at him, tried to pull him closer but he wormed from my reach. He was thin and lithe and he moved fluidly. He stood on the bed and beckoned me as he stretched languidly against one of the posts.

His erection tented his briefs. I crawled on hands and knees until I perched on my knees, his crotch at eye level. I slipped fingers up his thigh, in under his briefs and teased his cock. Leaning in, I kissed him through the fabric. His scent was intoxicating. Precum darkened the fabric and I tongued it then tugged abruptly at his waistband until his cock bounced free. My erection stirred as I wrapped a hand around the base of his hot pulsing cock. I could feel the internal tug of it as he reacted to my touch. I nudged his balls with my nose, inhaling deeply and then I tongued them, listening as he whimpered. Those whimpers alone nearly brought me to another orgasm. He shuddered as I took the head of his cock in my mouth. He tried to thrust but I pressed him back against the post. He drove fingers through my hair and pulled my face into his crotch. I tried not to gag as his cock slid across my tongue to the back of my throat. Again he whimpered. I grabbed his hands and held them at his side as he fucked my mouth. When he tried to pull out, I grabbed his ass and buried my face to the hilt and worked him back and forth. He pulled at my hair, trying to keep from coming but to no avail. I felt his cock swell and pulled off just enough so that I could taste his cum. I suckled his head and he writhed against the sensation, pushing at me to release him. When I finally did, he sank to his knees and kissed me. But I wasn't done. My cock was painfully firm. I pushed him onto his stomach and teased his hot pink hole with the head of my cock. I pushed a finger in and he moaned. His ass clamped down on it. It was more than I could take. I pressed into him, feeling the tightness envelop my cock. He was so wet. He pushed back and I slid further and deeper into him. Ashton's face was buried in a pillow but I heard him muttering. He reached back with one hand and gripped me by the ass and slammed me deeper into him. I laid on top of him and ground in deep and his muttering became guttural cries of ecstasy. He grunted with each thrust and whimpered as I withdrew only to drive back in again. He turned his head to kiss me hungrily, moaning into my mouth. Sweat plastered his hair to his forehead. He stared at me, into me, appearing mesmerized, but he gritted his teeth, looking almost feral. He pushed back to meet my thrusts. He tucked one of my arms under his chin and held on firmly as I fucked him harder and harder. He clamped his chin down and I felt his orgasm as his ass clinched tightly onto my cock. I roared, fighting against the climax, but after three more thrusts I came. I plunged into him. I cried out with each surge. We lay there in the dark, the moonlight glistening on sweat slick skin, breathing back to life. In that moment, I remembered something from my French class in high school. The French word for orgasm is le petit mort: *the little death. Certainly no words were ever so true. I watched Ashton open and close his eyes as if he were awakening for the first time. The smile that blossomed on his lips was catastrophically beautiful.*

Emily stared at me wide eyed, her jaw dropped.

"And then we cuddled." I finished.

It felt really hot all of the sudden and Emily still hadn't said anything. I picked up her empty cup and brought it to the kitchen, putting it in the sink. I looked in the refrigerator for something to snack on. I was feeling a bit peckish. "Hey Em. You hungry?"

I looked into the living room across the breakfast bar. Em was looking at me, the proverbial wheels turning. Then she frowned. "What?"

"Nothing." She rolled her eyes. "It's just. Why the hell couldn't you be straight? Good God almighty. I think I came just sitting here listening!"

I looked at her and grinned. "You're welcome."

CHAPTER SIXTEEN

Hitting the Mark

I stretched as Professor Meowington watched from his perch, the disdain in his eyes blatantly obvious. Emily called him a terrorist, which I thought was a bit of an over reaction to the time she helped me take him to the vet and he beheaded her *America* Beanie Baby. I tried to cast blame elsewhere until he hacked up the red white and blue ribbon from around its neck onto her leather seat. Suggesting it was just his social commentary about societies willingness to buy the most inane of objects resulted in me being pelted by said headless Beanie baby. Admittedly, Emily was a dog person and so didn't pick up on the subtle little nuanced behaviors of cats. She currently had an adorable cocker spaniel that was about as subtle as a brick through a plate glass window.

"Are you hungry?'

I got a little meow from him as he jumped down off the counter and went to his bowl. He meowed again, a little more insistently.

"I'm coming. I'm coming. Furry little ingrate." I stroked his fur as he wove in and out between my legs. He meowed in outrage as I nearly tripped over him reaching for the Meow Mix. "Well if you'd get out of my way." I nudged him with my foot.

Professor Meowington was the store cat. The owner had found him in the alley behind the store under the communal dumpster. She'd nursed him back to health and he's lived in the store ever since. Cleaning his kitty litter was an official employee duty. Dog people need not apply.

"Excuse me." A woman burdened with an armload of paperbacks stood at the cash counter. "Do you have baskets?"

I reached behind me and grabbed one of the blue baskets. She thanked me as I answered the phone

"Thank you for calling The Book Mark, where reading starts, how can I help you?" I listened half-heartedly as some kid asked about a book on his school reading list. "Did you need a particular edition…Uh huh…we have it in paperback and hardcover but yeah the paperback is cheaper… I'll be happy to hold you a copy...Certainly… We'll have it at the cash register for you...And your name?...Thank you."

I looked up and Aiden was standing at the counter. I fought the urge to smile with every fiber of my being.

"What are you doing here?"

"I need a book." He grinned and I felt myself warming to him instantly.

I looked at him dubious.

"What? I read."

"What's the last thing you read?" I put my elbows on the counter and put my chin in my hands.

"You'd be amazed at what goes into a box of Honey Nut Cheerios. Personally I think it's the tripotassium phosphate that really makes it zing."

Did I mention he has dimples? I rolled my eyes. "Book. The last *book* you read. And no, Dr. Seuss doesn't count."

He started to respond, opening his mouth, and then closing it abruptly. "You have to admit, One Fish Two Fish Red Fish Blue Fish *is* a classic." He straightened a stack of bookmarks with our store name and address on them, picking one up and pretended to read it.

"Aiden?"

He looked up seeming surprised that I was there.

"What do you want?" I inquired.

"I miss you."

"Aiden…"

"I mean we spent practically every day together for over a month and then all of the sudden, you're gone. I miss you." The second I miss you was a bit quieter than the first, but his eyes spoke volumes.

"Aiden…"

"Can't we go back to being friends? Just pretend nothing else happened. I didn't kiss you. We didn't have," he paused and looked around. "Well you know."

"No." I had to shut this down.

"No? No what? We can't go back? We can't be friends? What?"

No. To all of it." I wondered how many people had ever said no to Aiden Pike. His reaction said very few.

"Why?" Aiden sounded pained.

"You think we can be friends? After what happened? Would you be friends with Sophie if you broke up."

"Sure, why not?" Aiden shrugged his shoulders like the whole notion was no big deal.

"Really?" I was doubtful.

"Anyway it's not the same."

"And that's why." I crossed my arms and sat down on the stool behind me. I patted my thigh and Professor Meowington jumped up into my lap. His purr was in overdrive, which was a little soothing considering the circumstances.

"Why? Why what?"

"That's why we can't go back. That's why we can't 'Just be friends'." I did the quotation marks and everything. I was feeling a little riled up. "It is the same. It's exactly the same. If you love someone, you love someone."

"Wait, what?" Aiden looked up sharply.

I froze. I just realized what I just said. "I meant." *Oh shit.* I watched the smile blossom on his face. "What I meant to say was…" *Oh shit.* It was his turn to prop his chin in his hands on the counter. Smug looked so good on him. *Oh shit. Bastard.* "You said you loved me. And then you said you meant it. And now you want to just be friends."

"Hmmmm." Was his only response. I didn't like the sound of that; a little too much satisfaction, for my liking. "Well, I suppose that's a good reason for why *I* can't go back to being friends." Aiden leaned forward. "And what's your reason?"

"I don't want to be your friend."

The phone rang before he could respond, but the expression on his face told me I had hit home. I watched him jam his hands into the pockets of his jacket. My eyes followed him as he wove through the fixtures in the store waiting for me to get off the phone. I was mesmerized as he paused in front of one book and then moseyed on before stopping in front of another. He picked up a paperback copy of A *Game of Thrones.* It was then I realized he wasn't stopping randomly, but in front of my employee recommendations. He looked up at me and caught me staring. I looked down and then back up only to catch him smiling.

He sauntered over to the counter again. "Hey friend." I don't know if he meant to wink, but he did. I still had the phone under my chin but I couldn't tell you when the customer had hung up. What power did he have over me? I fought the longing. I shook my head trying to clear the images behind my eyes. A glistening wet Aiden Pike was not a good deterrent to the thought processes that were currently wreaking havoc with my psyche.

"Look Aiden." I swear if I say his name one more time...

"Are you okay?" Wait...It's PESD, isn't it? Heard of that?"

I couldn't help myself. I burst out laughing. I clapped a hand over my mouth. His timing was perfect, but the fact that he remembered what I had said the first time we kissed, made me swoon. Good lord, but I was boy crazy. What other explanation was there? I had to get rid of him before I broke. "Aiden, you need to leave."

"Let me come over after you get off..." He paused for affect. "...Work."

His mischievous grin battered my resolve. I came around the counter and did the last thing I should have done. I reached out to guide him towards the exit. He leaned into me and inhaled deeply, a hand on my shoulder. I nearly crumpled but he was quick to put a hand on my waist holding me against him. I laid my forehead on his shoulder whispering to myself. "Oh shit. Oh shit. Oh shit." I was shaking my head, or maybe I was just burrowing my face into the warm crook of his neck. "Aiden." I pleaded in a whisper. My arms snaked into the warmth under his jacket "Please Aiden. I can't do this. Everything is so..."

"It's just you. Just you and me." His words were a sibilant whisper. Or a memory, I wasn't certain.

I shook my head again. I didn't want to mention her name. I didn't want to acknowledge her in this moment. Not out loud.

"Cody." I shuddered at my name, feeling his breath tickle the base of my neck. "No, Cody."

I looked up at him, oblivious of everything else around me. He motioned with his eyes behind me. I turned. The customer with all the books was standing at the cash counter, glaring in our direction. I pulled away from him. His hands lingered on me, slipping down my back slowly until it was just his fingers, and then nothing.

I stood behind the counter, my cheeks and ears warm. I was certain they were red. The customer looked at me expectantly. I looked through her and deadpanned. "Dead relative."

She hefted her basket of books onto the counter with a heavy thud. "Yeah it looked real emotional." She glowered. I don't know why they don't let us beat the customers.

I started scanning her books, glancing over at Aiden.

"You scanned that one already."

"Oh I'm sorry." I think I could have spat on her and it would have been more genuine.

I watched her leave until my eyes landed on Aiden. I could tell he was laughing, even though he was turned away from me. I went over and stood behind him, jabbing him in the side. "Get out."

"Another satisfied customer." He laughed aloud this time and leaned back against the shelves. He put his hands on my waist and pulled me closer to him. "So?"

"Aiden." I whined.

"I'm not giving up on you." He ran his hands up and down my sides. "You might as well give in. Admit defeat. Come over to the dark side."

"Nerd."

"Unless you say otherwise, I'm gonna take that flagrant attack against my jock status as a yes."

"Fine. You win. But..."

"I'll be good." He crossed a finger over his heart like he had done before.

That's what worries me.

CHAPTER SEVENTEEN

Crazy

Girls are crazy. I knew Emily would take this badly. She's really a big baby. Sure tough prickly exterior, but on the inside she's a romantic marshmallow, all sweet gooey goodness.

"But." It's like she couldn't wrap her mind around it. "What about me?"

I had to do a double take like I didn't hear what she just said. "Whaaaaaaat?" I couldn't help laughing.

"Don't laugh at me Cody Beaumont!"

"What do you mean, what about you? I mean sure it'll be tough to do without all the vicarious Ashton love."

"That's not what I meant and you know it. I got you two together." She stamped her foot. "You have a responsibility."

"We've only been on one date. Had sex once." I pretended to pop my collar. "Granted it was all night long, but still, just once." I couldn't help but grin. "Don't look at me like that." I sat her on the couch and bent down on my knees in front of her. "Em. It's not a big deal. Ashton and I are dating. We're not exclusive. He knows all about Aiden."

"Aiden's gonna hurt you. He's already hurt you. But he's gonna hurt you again."

I nodded my head. "You're right."

She nodded more insistently. I loved her protective nature. Her steely resolve.

"But."

"Nope." She held up a hand to shut me up. "There's no room for buts."

I grinned.

"I'm serious Cody.   You're gonna give him another chance. And he's *going* to hurt you. Again!"

"Em.   I know you have my best interest at heart.   And I appreciate it. I do. But I have to do this."

"What about Ashton?"

"I like Ashton.   You know I do.   He's funny, smart and gorgeous. He's perfect."

Emily scooted up to the edge of the sofa. "So? Okay. Why don't you pick him? You said he's perfect."

"Too perfect."

"How can somebody be *too* perfect? Perfect is perfect. You can't be too perfect."

I sighed, frustrated.   "Em. Seriously. Just be happy for me. Okay? Let me try and be happy. If Aiden hurts me, then he hurts me."

"But…"

I took her hands in mine. "Em, all I know is if I don't, I'm always going to wonder." I looked down at our hands, my thumb playing across the back of her hand. "You didn't see his face when you went after him.   He never looked away.   He thought…he thought he deserved it."

"He did. He made you cry. He deserves a lot worse."

I squeezed her hands. "He was up there, telling me he loved me. That he meant it. And I told him no. And you hit him for it. You hit him for telling me he loved me.   Imagine that for a moment. I didn't know if I'd see him again."

I heard a sniffle. I looked up, surprised to see tears in her eyes, one glistening it's way down her cheek. I pulled her into a hug.

"You suck."   She sniffed and then rubbed her nose on my shoulder. "I can't believe you just made me the bad guy."

"I know. I know. I'm a bastard." I hugged her tighter. "But you still love me."

"True. Oh my god, I can't even face him." She returned the hug. "I'm leaving before he gets here.   Call me if you need me." She grabbed up her things and was out the door before I could say anything else. Maybe she was bipolar.

I must have fallen asleep on the couch afterwards because the next thing I heard was breaking glass. I woke with a start and looked around. At first I thought it was part of a dream then heard it again. I jumped up from the couch and looked out the peephole then ran to my balcony and looked out. Down below, swinging an aluminum bat at the passenger side window of my car was Sophie. *What the fuck?*

"Hey! What the fuck!" I ran through the apartment and scrambled down the stairs until I was in the parking lot. I watched helplessly as she swung again, knocking my rearview mirror halfway across the lot. "What the fuck are you doing?"

Sophie pulled the bat back for another swing at my car but then turned towards me and hurled the bat. I ducked and heard it hit the brick wall behind me. It clattered to the sidewalk that ran in front of the building.

"You know, he was just fine. Just fine before you." Sophie Savage was really beautiful. Maybe not right now, but I could easily see why Aiden was attracted to her. She was breathing heavily as she glared at me. I guess beating a FIAT with a baseball bat is exhausting.

Of course I knew who *he* was. "What are you talking about?"

"Stay away from him."

I could play and look stupid with the best of them. "Who?"

I'm not really that familiar with crazy. Sure I've seen it on TV, but not in real life. When she rushed me, I stumbled back caught completely unaware. The bushes broke my fall, as I clambered back away from her. She slapped at me and I felt her nails clawing at my neck and cheek. I scrambled back to my feet. I latched onto her wrists and she started kicking at me. We looked like we were doing some sort of crazy jig, her kicking towards my shin, me throwing my leg back out of reach. She connected a few times and it hurt like hell. The temptation to hit her, just once, was so strong; I can't even begin to describe it.

"Sophie. Stop!"

We were both breathing heavily.

"Look. I can't..."

"If you don't stay away, I'll out him. To everyone."

I was stunned silent. "Why would you..."

"I'm serious. I'll out him to everyone. Even his own mother will hate him."

"Do you know how crazy that sounds? Why would you hurt him like that? He loves you." It hurt to say those words. I didn't know if they were true, but certainly he had some feelings for her.

"You have no idea what you're talking about." There was so much anger in her voice, in her eyes. I'm sure if I didn't have her by the wrists she would have slapped me again. She smiled then, a wicked malicious smile. "You're not the first one, you know." She started laughing at my reaction. "Oh my God. You didn't know. You thought you were *the one*." She yanked her wrists from my grasp. "His precious little Cody." She said it under her breath as she rubbed her wrists. She eyed me up and down with disdain. "Have you ever wondered why he's never taken you home? All your little play dates at your place, not *one* at his. He's using you. Just like he's used all the rest. Just like he's using me."

All the rest? I stepped back from her, shaking my head, unwilling to accept what she was saying.

She was staring off; looking at nothing. "This little love affair of yours is over." She said it simply, like it was a done deal. "Break it off.

CHAPTER EIGHTEEN

This Little Love Affair

"Break it off."

The words continued to ring through my head. I sat on my bed, in the dark, my knees pulled up to my chest. I was done crying. I was done being mad. I was just done. I had called the police and reported my car vandalized, pretty much lying my ass off; no I didn't have any enemies, no I couldn't think of *anyone* who would want to do this to me. My description of the assailant was vague and completely off base. The idea of telling them *my gay lover's girlfriend nearly beat the shit out of me* was far too much for my pride to take. I took pictures of Carlo (really my FIAT's name was Charlie, but you know, he's Italian) and I sent them to my insurance agent along with my police report. I cradled the rearview mirror in my arms as I complained to the apartment manager, expressing utter outrage and alarm that just anyone could come into our gated community and destroy property with impunity. On the inside, I sighed with relief. Their apology and more importantly, the discount on my rent *almost* put a smile on my face.

I didn't dare call Emily. She would definitely kill Sophie. No doubt in my mind. And me, I was definitely contemplating a little murder myself. I had carefully stowed the aluminum bat in the back of my walk-in closet with thoughts of retribution floating around in my head. Certainly I wouldn't hit *her* with it. My mama raised me right. But I had no aversion to beating the shit out of her black BMW. That idea didn't bother me in the least.

What bothered me was the veracity of Sophie's words. Was she telling the truth? Was she lying? *Were* there others? Was

Chance McAvoy the latest in a string of guys? Or was I? Who else was there? I couldn't help but think back to my impression; that first kiss, how he was so at easy with it all. I banged my head back against the headboard. I didn't know what I was going to do.

My phone chirped happily from the nightstand. According to the installed app, the people who were going to replace my windshield were en route. I hopped up and ran to the bathroom. I looked wrecked. The scratches on my face and neck were an angry red and somehow I had picked up what looked like the beginnings of a black eye. My earlobe looked like a piercing gone horribly wrong. I splashed cold water on my face and ran fingers through my hair in an effort to make myself presentable. I stripped off the blood stained t-shirt and threw it in the hamper.

An urgent pounding on the door cut short my efforts. The door opened before I could get to it. Aiden stood in the doorway.

"What happened to your car?" It was out before he saw my face. "Oh my God, Beaumont! What happened?"

I shook my head, unable to find the words. It looked like he had just come from working out. He was freshly showered, his hair still damp. He wore a black tank top and running shorts with a white stripe down the side. I looked down at the stripe as his fingers floated atop the scratches on my cheek. "Who? Who did this to you?"

I shook my head again. "It's okay. I'm fine. It was nobody. You saw Carlo. Some…guys were taking a bat to him." I held up the rearview mirror. "Knocked one of his ears off." I said, mournfully. "I think they thought I was someone else." The lie came so easily.

"But your face." He pivoted my head up and looked at the scratches on my neck, hissing when he saw them.

"I tried to take the bat away. Didn't work out like I planned." I shrugged away from his touch and walked into the kitchen. "You want something to drink? We can order pizza if you want." I pulled a coupon from under a magnet on the refrigerator and waved it like it was a winning lottery ticket. "Any Pizza, any toppings, only ten dollars." I pulled open the refrigerator, pretending to search for something."

"Cody?"

I popped my head up over the door. "Huh?" I smiled halfheartedly.

"Why are you lying to me?"

Oh. That was rich. I was lying to him? "What?"

"You're lying." He had walked into the kitchen and cornered me against the refrigerator and the wall.

"Why would I lie?" I tried to duck around him but he grabbed me and pulled me into an embrace.

"You can tell me. Anything." Pressed against his chest, I could feel his heart beat. My arms hung slack against my side. I couldn't bring myself to hug him back. If I did I wouldn't let go. If I did, I wouldn't be able to do what I had to do.

"Aiden. I don't think this is going to work." There was no conviction in my voice.

"What?" The look in his eyes tore at me. I forced myself to continue. "You and me. I just don't think... I've thought about it... I just... damn it." I scrubbed at my eyes, fighting back tears. "What you want and what I want aren't the same."

"Cody. What's wrong? Everything was fine this afternoon. We were fine. I felt it. *You* felt it. Don't tell me you didn't."

"I... I just got caught up in the moment. I wasn't expecting to see you." I tried to walk around him again but Aiden blocked my escape.

"No. Damn it Cody. No. You love me." He was so insistent, so certain but pleading for validation. The truth of his words struck me. He took my hands and held them to his chest, tapping above his heart. "Say it. Say you love me."

I tried to pull my hands from his grip, tried to pull away from him, but he held strong, pulling me closer to him. I shook my head, closing my eyes. I couldn't look at him. I couldn't lie to him. Not about this.

"Cody. Please."

"It was Sophie." I said it as coldly and dispassionately as I could.

Aiden froze. "What?"

"Sophie. She did it. My car. My face." I pushed away from him. He still hadn't moved. He was staring straight ahead, through me; the look on his face: submission, resignation, defeat. I took another step back.

"Cody. I can explain."

"Is it true?" Aiden said nothing, just looked at me, his eyes pleading. "Is it true?"

His response, whatever it might have been was cut short by a knock at the door.

The windshield repair specialist (that's what his card said) shook my hand. "You have any problems, be sure and call me. You can call the number on the card or call your insurance agent and they can get in touch with us." He handed me another card and pointed at the missing rearview mirror. "They can fix that. Good as new. No one'll ever know the difference."

"Thanks."

I had left Aiden in the kitchen accompanying the repairmen downstairs. Clearly this was not his first car beating. He whistled in appreciation. I watched with disinterest as he removed the damaged windshield and replaced it with a new one. He pulled out the passenger side window and replaced it as well. All the while I was glancing back over my shoulder up at my balcony. I saw Aiden once, peering out of the dark. I quickly looked away.

I spent another ten minutes sitting on the front steps flipping the business cards over and over in my hand, unwilling to go up, to face the truth. Admittedly, I wanted to believe the best. But history had proven too many times, that the best was never even remotely within reach. I opened my front door hesitantly. I didn't see Aiden in the living room. I took a deep breath and stepped in, feeling like an invader in my own home. "Aiden?" My voice sounded alien. I cleared my throat. "Aiden?"

I stopped and peered into the bathroom. A bloody towel lay on the counter from my earlier ministrations. I dropped it in the hamper covering my blood stained t-shirt. "Aiden?" My voice echoed in the bathroom. I felt a moment's trepidation. I turned to the bedroom, my heart beating a little more strongly. It was dark in there, the curtains heavy thick fabric that kept the sun at bay. I saw Aiden on my bed. He was curled almost in a fetal position. In his arms, one of my pillows, held tightly. I could scarcely hear him breathing. I stepped in tentatively and stood at the foot of the bed. I watched him, his lashes fluttering as he dreamed.

Damn it.

I kicked my shoes off and climbed up on the bed and curled up next to him. I draped an arm over him and he latched onto it pulling me tighter against him. "Aiden?" I whispered and he stirred in his sleep. I kissed the back of his neck, just below his ear. I watched for any reaction. I leaned in closer to him, my lips barely touching his ear. "I love you."

CHAPTER NINETEEN

Wilde & Free

Some time in the night we had changed positions and now he spooned me, his arm draped over me. He had removed his tank top and my shirt. His warm chest pressed against my back was comforting. His voice vibrated in his chest, a subtle purr. "Do you remember the first time we met?" Aiden asked.

I nodded, the grin on my face, an unconscious response. I rested back against him and he embraced me tighter. "I honestly think, that *that* was the moment I fell for you." I turned towards him. He reached up and covered my eyes. I smiled, my hand covering his. "Will you let me tell it, without looking at me?" I nodded again and turned back around, tucking our hands together against my chest. I closed my eyes.

"You know, it wasn't the first time I saw you. Well it was, but not what you think. The park, you walk through the park to work sometimes. Me and some of the guys were playing football. Well really we were just throwing the ball around when I saw you. You had that ugly backpack on…"

I laughed aloud and elbowed him. "I loved that back pack. It had character."

"It was ugly. Really ugly." I could hear the smile in his voice and wanted nothing more than to see it. "Anyway, you were wearing that backpack, with all the jangling chains and buttons and stickers. You'd never be able to sneak up on anyone with that thing on."

"Hey, I've got ninja skills." He covered my mouth. I bit at his palm.

"Shhhhh. Let me tell it." He kissed the back of my neck, a quick peck. "Anyway, ugly backpack, that red tank with the hello kitty writing on it and those shorts." He squeezed me, his crotch pressed ever so subtly against my backside. I got the impression he liked those shorts

"I guess you were off that day, but I watched you as you walked across the park and along the sidewalk, window shopping and guy watching. I saw you stop and turn and watch this group of guys who had just passed you. You were fearless. One of them looked back and you waved before whirling back around like some diva."

"Hey!"

"No. It was so cute. You have no idea. I couldn't take my eyes off of you. It was only like a minute, maybe two that it took you to walk down the sidewalk, but I lost track of everything." Aiden chuckled softly to himself. "I remember Billy Blaylock ran up next to me and started looking, wondering what hot chick I was staring at. I was so captivated, you had already gone into the bookstore and I was still staring after you."

"You're making me blush." I buried my face in my pillow, a silly grin on my face.

"What? It's true. Blaylock had to shove me to bring me back to reality. I was completely gone. They threatened to tell Sophie. Of course they had no idea."

"I passed that bookstore I don't know how many times. I walked back and forth but I couldn't work up the nerve to go in. I was afraid you'd see me, and see right through me. That first time, after we were done playing football in the park, we all went our separate ways and I stopped by that big bay window. You had this big John Green display of books. I remember how much I loved that one book, *Looking for Alaska.*" Aiden laughed again, this time a little louder. "I was having this whole conversations in my head about what I was going to say if you came out. But then I saw you. You were sitting on one of those bean bag chairs in the kids section with *that cat.*"

"Professor Meowington." I corrected.

"Yes, Professor Meowington."

There was so much disdain in his voice I couldn't help but burst out laughing.

"I could have sworn at one point you saw me so I ran. I ran as fast as I could till I got to the CVS on the corner." Aiden rolled away from me onto his back. I felt his fingers playing on my hip, tracing circle eights along the waistband of my shorts. "I was…" I heard him shaking his head, his hair whispering against the pillow. "I was such a stalker for like two weeks. Then we had to get copies of To Kill a Mockingbird for my English Lit class." He rolled back onto his side and I welcomed the contact. I snuggled back against him. He was fidgeting. "If it wasn't for English Lit..."

"I remember you coming in. I remember the bell over the door ringing. I remember looking up. Like in the movies. All slow motiony. And I saw you and... No I'm not even going to say it." I was completely and totally smitten.

Aiden kissed the back of my neck again and I felt him smile then he shhhhhshed me.

"Let me finish." He sighed deeply against my neck. "Sophie was with me. She was pissed about something. I don't know what. She wass always pissed about something. The last thing I wanted was for the two of you to be in the same room." He was playing with my hair, running fingers through it as he spoke.

"Why?"

His fingers stopped moving for a moment. "She knew. She knew everything."

This time I did turn. His pained expression tore at my heart. "What do you mean, she knew?"

"I mean, she knew I was gay. She's known almost as long as I have." He closed his eyes. "She...we've known each other since like sixth grade. She was my first girlfriend. But it didn't feel right. Or," He paused as if considering his words. "I guess I didn't know what right was supposed to feel like. We tried being boyfriend and girlfriend and I pretended for a long time. We kissed. We had...sex. We did everything normal couples were supposed to do. But..." Aiden shook his head. "She asked me junior year if I was gay. I didn't talk to her for like almost a month. I felt so small. Deceitful. I had these anxiety attacks, I couldn't breathe, I couldn't..."

I kissed him. Or I tried to but he pulled away, our lips barely grazing.

"Anyway. At the bookstore, she guessed almost right away. She wanted to order the books online, but I insisted on going to the bookstore. I swear I almost had an attack in the car. I was fidgeting and nervous and couldn't breathe. I almost changed my mind, pretended I'd forgotten my wallet, but she said we were already there so she'd buy the books. I hoped and prayed it was your day off. But, there you were. Perched on top of that stool, *that cat* in your lap."

"Professor Meowington." I corrected again.

"You looked up and smiled and I was..." He was smiling as he remember . then the smile vanished. "I remember Sophie...God she was so jealous, it's like she smelled it in the air. She hooked an arm through mine and pulled me tight against her, she even went so far as to tuck my shoulder in between her boobs. Even though she knew boobs held no power over me. I didn't even know you were gay. But I think Sophie's gaydar was fine tuned."

I smiled wryly. "I remember her asking for Oscar Wilde. Asking me if I knew Oscar Wilde. Telling me I *had* to know Oscar Wilde. I remember thinking she was a little bit crazy and that the guy she was with was hot as hell." I laughed into his chest as he looked at me. He didn't get it. "Oscar Wilde is like one of *the* iconic gay authors. *Picture of Dorian Gray? The Importance of Being Earnest?*" No reaction. "Philistine."

"What? I don't read." He countered.

I sighed dramatically. "Don't remind me."

"Anyway..." He stared into my eyes, his finger played down my cheek, traced my jawline. "I don't know why she reacted so differently to you. She was very derogatory. She griped about the way you walked, the way you talked, the way you flirted with me."

"I didn't flirt with you!" I was *almost* certain I didn't.

"She said you gave me your bedroom eyes." He smiled gleefully as I glared. "As far as she was concerned, we were never going to your bookstore again."

I rolled my eyes.

"She was so hateful. Not just towards you. But me too. I mean after I told her the truth, we pretended to still be together. She said it was a win-win situation..."

"Oh my gosh, you used her line on me." I feigned outrage.

"Oh hush. We'd been hanging out for weeks. I couldn't wait any more. I didn't want to wait."

I blinked over at him.

"She hated you. The first time you and I hung out; just the two of us. We saw *A Good Day to Die Hard.*"

"Don't remind me. Even you have to admit it was horrible."

He grinned at me, his eyes distant. "I don't even remember it. I remember your arm touching mine on the armrest, how warm it was and soft. I remember your lips were so shiny from the buttered popcorn. I remember wanting to kiss you. I remember dropping you off at your apartment and sitting in the car afterwards wondering what the hell I was doing and telling myself I couldn't do this."

"We didn't even talk for like a week after that." My voice held a hint of accusation.

"I was determined to stay away. Sophie, she hated you so *she* was ecstatic. She made plans every day. Anything to keep me away from you. She intentionally didn't drive anywhere near your bookstore. My eyes would wander down the exit on the freeway that led to your work and I swear I felt the car speed up. Out of sight, out of mind as far as she was concerned.

Meanwhile, I'm stalking you on the internet." Aiden blushed adorably. "Facebook Twitter. I found your Vine. The one where you and Emily are singing. Oh my God you were so cute." Aiden threw his head back against his pillow and sighed. "I googled you for hours."

"Kinky." I laughed into my hand as he hushed me again.

The anxiety I felt when Aiden first started talking was gone. I was lying on his chest, my head on his shoulder. He continued playing with my hair.

"Sophie said…" Did I want to know the truth?

"What?"

"That there were others. That I wasn't your first." I sat up and turned around, gazing directly at him. "You wanted to know what all the fuss was about, remember?"

He blinked at me, starting to reply. His lips parted, then closed. He sat up and leaned back against the headboard. He took my hand and played with my fingers. "I…" He shook his head with a wry grin. "I'm not bragging, I swear, but I've kissed a lot of guys."

I started to pull my hand away but he held onto it and quickly continued. "I've kissed a lot of guys and a lot of girls. But I've never kissed anyone I had feelings for. A kiss was just a kiss, until I kissed you. That's why Sophie hated you. That's why she hates you. Because I love you."

I guess I looked dubious.

"You don't believe me." He shrugged his shoulders and looked down. "You can ask her. I told her. After I talked to you at the bookstore. I told her. She went ballistic. Started throwing shit. Threatened to tell everyone I was a fag. Told me how disgusting I was, how it made her sick." He was looking at our hands, kept folding my fingers into a fist and then unrolling each finger like he was counting. Then he looked up again, tears in his eyes. "Have you ever cried because you were so happy and so sad at the same time?" He wiped at his eyes, but smiled. "The only two times I've ever admitted loving someone and I get racked in the balls by your best friend and hated by my...by Sophie."

I stood up on my bed and offered him my hand. "Come on."

He looked up at me puzzled. "What? Where we goin'?"

"I'm gonna make it up to you." I offered him my other hand and pulled him up till we were face to face, standing on my bed.

"And how are you going to do that?" He leaned closer to me.

"Easy." Without losing eye contact, I slipped my shorts down and stepped out of them. Coming back up I cupped his cock and balls. His eyes got real big and he smiled. "I'm going to take a shower."

"Uh huh?"

"And I'm gonna let you get all the hard to reach places." I smiled and stepped off the bed. For a moment I felt his eyes on me, then I heard him bounding off the bed after me.

CHAPTER TWENTY

Table for Three

"Story tiiiiiiiime." Emily was a kid in the proverbial candy store. Her giddiness was off the scale as she bounced up and down in the booth like a kid hopped up on sugar. I suspected she was really waiting to hear about one thing and one thing only, but I was going to make her wait. Not so much to torture her, but that was part of it. "Em, you're gonna need to conserve your energy."

Emily leaned back in her seat, taking deep breaths. "I can't help it." Another deeper breath. "I mean, if you want the truth, I don't believe it. It sounds a bit…"

"What?" This should be good.

"Well, to be honest. You're a bit of a goody two shoes."

I feigned indignation. It was true, though. And I didn't really have a problem with being "a good guy" but being a bad guy seemed to have its perks. Okay, maybe I was stretching the definition of bad guy since I really didn't do anything, but still, after last night. "You can't tell anyone. I'm serious. Em, if I hear so much as a peep."

Emily mimed the whole 'cross my heart, hope to die, stick a needle in my eye' routine followed by her locking her lips and throwing away the key bit.

"We agreed I could tell you, because I can't keep a secret from you." Emily nodded, not in agreement, but rather with a menacing expression that said, you better not keep secrets from me.

I rolled my eyes.

"So tell me, already."

I sat back and looked at her. Where to start? I'd already told her about pyscho Sophie, about poor Carlo, (I wouldn't have another rearview mirror for at least a week), about Aiden. I didn't tell her about the shower. Aiden had given me a thorough scrubbing.

"Hey! No cheating. Anything that makes you smile like that, you're supposed to share with me. That's the rule."

"The rule?"

"Yes. The rule."

"Is it one of those unspoken Emily rules? You know the ones I don't know about yet because you haven't told me?"

"Maybe. If you were a little more forthcoming I wouldn't have to throw these rules in your face."

"So it's my fault?"

Emily sighed shaking her head with contrived disappointment. "Cody Cody Cody. What's rule number one?"

I laughed. "You're always right."

"And rule number two?"

"It's always my fault." I spoke robotically.

"Need I say more?" She drank noisily.

"No, I think you've said enough."

"Good. Now, about that threesome?"

I cackled with embarrassed laughter. Emily was so brazen and tactless. It wasn't really a threesome. Okay, technically it was.

Aiden walked fingers across my hip. Our shower was a brilliant success. I can't honestly say I'd never felt cleaner, but he did manage to get all the hard to reach places. I was becoming a staunch proponent of shower sex. Maybe it was the steam, the hot water cascading off of hard bodies, the intimacy of being pressed against the cold tile, my hands forced above my head as he thrust into me, filling me. Maybe it was the acoustics of the shower, his moans and groans, my whimpering and cries, an audio soundtrack to our lovemaking. I was hard just thinking about it. Aiden leaned and kissed my swollen cock head.

"Oh my. What are you thinking about?"

"You have to ask?"

We were both blushing. He walked his fingers across my hips again and further up my side. I squirmed at the sensation. It tickled. I grabbed his hand and rolled away from him, laughing. "Stop." I pleaded. Aiden's eyes sparkled. He jumped up and straddled me. I stared up at him, breathing heavily. We were both hard. I grabbed his dick and he thrust his hips. He teased my

*nipples, pinching them lightly. He played fingers under my arms.
I held them flush against my sides to keep him from tickling me.
His fingers were digging into my sides mercilessly. I shrieked with
laughter and tried to buck him off. I begged and pleaded for him
to stop. I struggled breathlessly, shaking my head back and forth.
Tears blurred my vision as I laughed. I held his wrists to no avail.
I squirmed and bucked with renewed effort.   He relented for a
moment to lean down to kiss me.   I wrapped my arms around his
neck and pulled him down. My heart was pounding, my dick hard
and slick. Aiden was a top, but all I could think about was being
inside of him. I could tell he knew what I was thinking because he
teased me, grinding his ass down on my cock. He was the devil.   I
bucked suddenly, catching him off guard and rolled out from under
him. I ran through the apartment, yelling at the top of my lungs.
My escape was only temporary as he grabbed me and we both fell
on the couch. He began tickling me again and I was yelling for
him to stop, flaying my arms wildly, kicking, I even tried to bite
him.*

*Before I knew it however, I was on the couch by myself. Ashton
stood in the middle of the living room. He had pulled Aiden off of
me and flung him across the room. I knew what it must have
looked like. I was yelling for Aiden to stop, I had scratches and a
black eye from Sophie. Aston took one look at me and threw
himself at Aiden.   They struggled for the upper hand, pressed
against the wall on the floor. Fists were flying. I tried breaking
them up, but was knocked backwards on my ass, for my trouble. I
don't think they heard me yelling for them to stop.   Aiden was
naked so every blow he received was an angry red blotch. Ashton
must have come straight from work. His apron was torn as well as
the white polo underneath it.   One of his shoes had come off as
they struggled and although he wore a belt, his khakis were
halfway off. I hate to admit it, but I was a little turned on.   I
grabbed Ashton's arm as he swung down at Aiden's face. I was
tossed forward over Ashton's shoulder and hit the wall. Ashton's
fist connected squarely with Aiden's jaw. Both of them looked
feral, teeth snarling, eyes wild, every muscle visibly taut and
straining as the wrestled. Aiden gave as well as he got, as blood
dripped from a cut above Ashton's eye and he had an angry welt
where they had both crashed against the coffee table.   I was
about to dive back into the fray when they both came tumbling
back at me. I found myself crushed between Ashton and the wall.*

The framed Nagel prints came crashing down, the glass shattering and skittering across the wooden floor.

"Hey." It's like I wasn't even here. "HEY!" Fuckers. I tried to pry myself between them, slipping an arm between them only to get stuck. The three of us teetered one direction and then rushed headlong in the other. I felt and heard the glass underfoot. I looked down and saw blood. Mine or maybe Aiden's as he too was trampling through the broken glass. He seemed oblivious. I was feeling faint, a bit nauseous. I yanked my arm from between them and stumbled backwards. I kept waiting to trip over the couch or hit the wall. It felt like I was stumbling for hours. I guess I fell. I guess I blacked out. I don't know. All I know is waking up in my bed. I looked around disoriented. I heard whispering beyond the closed door. I sat up. Aiden or Ashton had covered me with a sheet, but my feet stuck out from the end, bandaged in gauze. I cringed, expecting pain as I wiggled my toes. Surprisingly, I felt nothing. I smiled sleepily and flung the sheet off. I was still naked underneath. For some reason I found that quite funny and couldn't help giggling. The whispering stopped and I heard footsteps. The door opened. Aiden and Ashton stood side by side, both of them beautiful though a little worse for wear. Both of them had cut lips and little Band-Aids covering scratches and cuts. Aiden was dressed again in his shorts and tank and Ashton was wearing my Paramore t-shirt. I waved, taking a moment to admire the way my fingers moved so fluidly through the air. Ashton smiled wryly.

"What?" My voice sounded foreign. "What? What? What?" I sounded different with each what. Weird.

This time Aiden smiled. "Are you feeling okay Beaumont?"

"Cody. You're supposed to call me Cody." I whined. I don't know why that was so important but I suddenly felt very emotional.

"I have to pee." I got up rather quickly and the room tilted to one side and I with it. "Weeeeeeeee."

Aiden and Ashton were at myself almost like magic. I had one arm over each of their shoulders. I lifted my feet and clung to them, hanging between them swinging back and forth. Something weird was going on. "To my throne." I bellowed and laughed, pointing with one finger and then the other. I saw bloody tissue in the waste basket. "Who got hurt?"

Aiden and Ashton looked at each other.

"What?" I looked from one lovely face to the other.

They propped me against the wall and I started sliding down or they were floating up. I wasn't quite sure until I was sitting on my ass staring up at them.

"I think you gave him too much." Aiden chastised. Aiden's lips made me want to kiss him. I could see one of his nipples peeking out from the tank top.

"It's the only thing I had." Ashton looked down at me too. I reached up and pulled on the t-shirt he was wearing.

"Only thing you had, what?" I covered my mouth, scandalized. "Oh my god. You ruffied me!"

They both laughed at that. Which pissed me off.

"Not fair. Not fair." I grabbed a handful of the t-shirt and yanked Ashton down onto his knees. I grabbed him by the back of the neck and pulled him into a kiss. With my other hand, I reached up and under the hem of Aiden's shorts and groped him.

Both of them reacted with surprise. Aiden tried to push my hand out from under his shorts. I had no choice but to pull them down. As usual, he was going commando. Ashton pulled back from my grasp, breaking the kiss. He fell onto his heels, which put him eye level to Aiden's hardening cock. Ashton watched mesmerized. I couldn't help laughing and climbed up off of my ass and inched over until I too was kneeling in front of Aiden. I kissed Ashton again, this time more softly. I reached blindly out for Aiden. I felt his ass, grabbed it and nudged him towards Ashton and me. Ashton resisted my direction as I shoved his face into Aiden. I rose up on my knees and leaned in and as I kissed the tip of Aiden's dick, I watched Ashton's lips work their way along the shaft. I kissed him and Aiden's dick at the same time. Our tongues mingled over the swollen pink head. I could taste Aiden; I could smell him, a subtle lust inducing scent that was driving me crazy. I pulled Aiden down to his knees. He crumpled easily and kissed me hungrily. Ashton had followed Aiden's dick lower and as I kissed Aiden, Ashton made him moan in my mouth as he sucked on Aiden's cock. I don't know why I was feeling cheated but I pulled Ashton off of Aiden and maneuvered his lips to my own cock. He kissed and lapped at it with his tongue and I couldn't help thrusting my cock past his lips. Aiden had his hand on the back of Ashton's head, pushing. My hips were thrusting on their own accord and Ashton pulled back, gagging for a moment before he plunged all the way down.

I was so close to an orgasm; it took all my willpower to push Ashton off of me. I rose up quickly and grabbed both of them by their hands and dragged them back to my bedroom. Ashton was still wearing his khakis. I pushed him on the bed and practically tore them off of him. He stared up at me his breathless, his cock pulsing. I helped him take off the t-shirt then fell on him, our cocks smashing together. I yelled, the sensation rocking my mind as my cock slipped between his thighs, right under his balls. He arched his back and tried to lift his legs but I wrestled him onto his stomach. Aiden was right behind me. I felt him stabbing at me. His cock was slick with precum and Ashton's spit. I reached back and gave his cock a couple of hard tugs and then maneuvered him until I felt his cock pushing at my hole. I felt him pushing into me and reached back further and pulled him hard against me. His cock filled me up and I collapsed on top of Ashton, my cock impaling him. The three of us yelled in unison; Ashton and I out of the sudden pain, but Aiden's was an animal's roar of lust and conquest. He pounded into me and I cried out with each thrust. The sensations were almost too much for me. Feeling Aiden buried deep in me, his thrusts forcing me deep into Ashton, the only sounds I could make were exquisite breathless sobs. I bit Ashton's shoulder, the back of his neck and he cried out. He turned and kissed me. He was pushing back to meet my thrusts and I felt my orgasm building. I pulled Ashton's hair, pulling his head back. I sucked and kissed his neck leaving a line of vibrant red marks. His back arched even more, his ass clinched down on my cock. Aiden's thrust became more frantic. He growled drowning out the slapping thrusts. I'm sure I climaxed first. I clamped my arms around Ashton and thrust deep inside of him and the force of my climax overwhelmed me. My ass fastened tightly around Aiden's cock. He bellowed to the ceiling as he lunged a final time and unleashed a flood of cum. I heard Ashton moan and his body strained against itself, every one of his muscles forced taut and I felt him thrusting against the mattress under me. I reached under him and grabbed his cock and he thrust into my grip. His cock was slick and I teased the head, pinching my fingers closed. His climax was punctuated by moaning sighs as he shot load after load into my palm. He shuddered when I continued stroking him. The three of us lingered like that, weak and breathing heavily, hearts beating wildly. Aiden wrapped his arms around me and I embraced Ashton.

"You lie!" Emily's ice cream had melted into a caramel vanilla mess.

I nodded, smiling. I knew my ears and cheeks were red Emily looked at me disbelieving. "You have got to be kidding me."

I nodded again.

"Seriously?" Emily shook her head. "Next time, and there better be a next time, bring a video camera.

I rolled my eyes. Admittedly, the idea was tantalizing.

CHAPTER TWENTY-ONE

Torn

I watched Ashton come through the employee door and hide his cigarettes in the cubbyhole at the service station.   His apron hung around his neck, the untied strings trailing behind him as he hurried to the bathroom.   I looked down at the table, drinking absently from my glass.   It took me a moment to realize I was writing the letters AP with my finger, in the condensation on the table, and another moment to realize that both Aiden and Ashton had the same initials.

Aiden Pike or Ashton Prince?

After our little *ménage à trois* I'd been giddy, not thinking about the ramifications.   I hadn't talked to either one of them in three days.   I'd picked up the phone on several occasions, even dialed their numbers but that's as far as I got.   I didn't know what to say. And neither one of them had called me.

The morning after was a little awkward.   Waking up, sandwiched between the two of them, Ashton's arm draped over my waist, his hand resting on Aiden's bare hip sent a wave of jealousy through me.   Ashton was spooning me and to put it plainly, it was morning and the wood was up.   I didn't dare move. He was grinding a little in his sleep, his morning hard-on nudging my left ass cheek.

Aiden slept peacefully.   And he was beautiful, his lips drew my eye; pouty perfection that begged to be kissed.   I could count his eyelashes; that's how close I was.   I drew a finger down the line of his neck to the shallow spot below his Adam's apple.   Aiden sighed sleepily, opened his eyes and I fell into them.   I couldn't help it. His smile melted me, his eyes closing just barely as he mouthed the words 'Good Morning' silently. He didn't seem to notice Ashton, which left me torn, and feeling guilty.

"*I'm sorry.*" I mouthed.

He squinted in confusion. "*For what?*" Then realization as he gaze shifted over my shoulder. He shook his head, rolling his eyes dismissively. "*Can we keep him?*"

I didn't mean to, but I barked out a laugh that shattered the silence. It startled Ashton so much that he grabbed Aiden and pulled him tight against me while simultaneously he thrust his still hard dick into my ass. I felt Aiden's hard-on slip exquisitely under my balls. I buried my face in the pillow suppressing a moan. I didn't realize just how big Ashton was. He hadn't fucked me but I'd had my hands on that thing and I was torn between reaching back and pulling him deeper into me or pushing him out. The pain was sublimely breathtaking. I curled my toes and tensed at the sudden invasion. He pulled out just as suddenly. I jumped out of bed, knees weak, wrapping myself with the sheet. Aiden stared up at me wide-eyed while Ashton slept peacefully.

"Hey." Ashton stood at my table his eyes sparkling. "What were you thinking about? Me, I hope." I blushed. Ashton slid into the booth next to me. He ran a hand up my thigh. "Am I crazy or were we...I don't know...it's like I can still feel it, feel you. And Aiden." He'd said that last part a little quieter and my fists clinched.

Was I jealous? And why? Was it that I only wanted Ashton for myself, or Aiden for myself? Or that I wanted to be the only one that Ashton thought of, that Aiden shouldn't even be an afterthought. It was really a bit too late for that.

I hated my insecurities. Hated feeling like I wasn't good enough. I felt like I was going to lose one of them; to the other. I don't know why. As far as I knew, they didn't know each other. But, was there something? The touches between them seemed too familiar, easily intimate, no hesitation.

"Hey. Where'd you go?"

I shook my head. "Just tired I guess."

"You hungry." He gave our surroundings a cursory once over. "It's on me."

I shook my head again. "I already ate. I just...I wanted to talk to you about...you know."

"Oooookay." Ashton slipped the little order pad into the pocket of his apron.

"It's nothing bad." I reassured him "I just need to talk about it. I'm a little…I dunno, screwed up in the head about it. I mean you, Aiden and me. I don't know."

"I can meet you at yours, if you want?" He looked at his watch. "But I don't get off until 5:00"

I nodded absently and finished my Dr. Pepper.

"You sure you don't want anything?"

"No I was just wanting to talk." Part of me wanted to stay. Part of me wanted his attention, his smile, his eyes lighting up for a moment every time he saw me. But it was like watching your favorite show on television and being interrupted by commercial breaks. I got up and he wrapped me in a hug, kissing me quickly on the lips. Before I could lean into it, before I could savor it, he rushed off to wait on a tableful of teenagers.

"Cody."

I turned and Ashton threw himself into my arms. Off balance, we both slipped back into the car and slid sideways until I caught myself on the hood. Ashton wrapped both arms around me and kissed me, planting kisses all over my face and lips. The last kissed was long and luxuriant, tender but impassioned, a hand pulling at my hair while his other arm was wrapped around my waist holding me tightly against him.

I took a deep breath when he pulled away from the kiss. "What? What was that for?"

He gestured towards the window and I looked. There were five faces expressing utter glee pressed to the large pane glass window. I looked back at Ashton and he smiled shyly. "They asked me if you were my boyfriend." He paused and looked down. "I told them yes." He grinned. "They told me to prove it."

I grabbed Ashton by his apron and pulled him into another kiss.

CHAPTER TWENTY-TWO

Broken

"I don't know what to do." I was pacing my apartment like a caged animal.

"He actually called you his boyfriend?" Emily had brought a new knitting project, a wooly pair of socks. They looked like a pair of smashed calico cats. I didn't have the heart to tell her knitting was not the way to go.

I nodded vigorously, unable to respond verbally.

"But you don't think he meant it? That it was just for show?"

"No." I shrugged, slumping down next to Emily on the couch. 'That's just it. I don't know. He seemed sincere. And I want him to be sincere. But… but…" I grabbed a ball of yarn and rolled it around in my hands

"But what about Aiden?"

I nodded

Her knitting needles clacked together as she knitted. "I swear. You get yourself into so much trouble. "

"This is your fault! You have to go and find me a guy that's perfect."

"Too perfect." Emily added wryly. She held up her knitting as a shield. "Your words, not mine."

I glared. "So what am I going to do?"

"Well." She concentrated on her knitting.

I leaned forward. "Well, what?"

"Well you're going to have to choose."

"Oh my god. Thank you for pointing out the obvious."

"Hey! Look. You put yourself in this situation. You had your chance to break it off with Aiden and you didn't. You wanted to break it off with Ashton and then you didn't. Then...then you have a threesome with them both. How is this my fault?"

"The threesome really wasn't my fault. And it was..."

"Stop. Don't even say another word. If I hear how perfect it was one more time, I'm going to knit your mouth shut." She pointed a knitting needle at me. "I don't get how *this* is making your life miserable. Seriously. Oh boo hoo! Poor poor Cody. How will you ever get by?"

"I never said my life was miserable." I shook my head. "I can't."

"You can't what?"

"I can't choose."

"Cody. You have to choose. It's not fair to them. You can't string them along. Ashton's already ...I know, I know, we don't know if he was serious, but he said it. And Aiden..."

"Said he loved me." Emily set her knitting in her lap and looked at me, her jaw open but without a response.

"Ashton's never said it." I continued. "Not once. Aiden's said it like half a dozen times now."

Emily sighed. "I don't know what to tell you Cody. I wish I did." She held up her socks and grimaced. One looked like it had room for three extra toes. "God these things are awful." She gathered everything up and shoved the whole mess into her canvas bag. "Look, maybe you need a break. No Aiden. No Ashton. Just Cody. And maybe a little Emily." She smiled. "We haven't had a road trip in a while." Her voice perked up. "I can trade with some people at work and we can go this weekend. Come on. Road trip!"

"Do you remember the last road trip?"

"That was a fluke. Plus you had the hots for that one guy, what was his name, Justin. If you would have told me beforehand I could have run interference. Instead, someone, I'm not gonna mention any names or point any fingers, but *someone* was the biggest bitch on the planet for 5 days. I swear I thought you were manstruating."

"On that note. You need to leave. Ash is gonna be hear soon and ..."

The knock at the door silenced both of us.

"A million dollars it's Aiden." Emily stifled laughter.

"You're evil." I whispered then opened the door.

Aiden leaned against the rail. He looked up as I opened the door. "Hey." He quirked a smile and took the two steps between us and wrapped me in his arms. A wave of fragrances overwhelmed me; cologne, a citrusy bodywash, and a coconut scented shampoo combined for a delicious aroma that made me want to bite him.

I cleared my throat. "Hey." I wrapped my arms tight around him and stood there breathing him in.

"I missed you." He whispered.

"Well I gotta go. See you two love birds later." Emily barged by us and down the stairs. "Tell Ashton, I said hi."

I glared over Aiden's shoulder as she skipped to her car. I'm pretty sure I was going to have to kill her. Maybe after the road trip.

"What's that all about?"

"Ashton's supposed to come over after he gets off work."

"Oh." I felt his arms slacken. *Shit.*

"I just needed to talk to him. About the other night. It was a little intense. The fight. The..." *sex.*

"Cody."

I pulled back so I could look him in the eyes.

"About Ashton. There's something I needed to tell you about him."

"Okay." This didn't sound good at all. His eyes held a hint of apprehension.

"How much do you know about Ashton?" Aiden leaned back against the doorframe.

"I don't know. Not very much really. We've only been out a couple of times. Emily kinda set me up with him at Chloe's party. Aiden was nodding; he knew all of this. "Why?

"Well before you and I...I mean...as far as sex, Aston and I, we...I mean it's not like it meant anything since I paid him, but we..."

"Wait.... what? You paid him?"

"I thought you knew."

"You thought I knew what. Ashton's a prostitute?"

"Was. He's not anymore. But, you've been to his place. You think he bought that working at the Frozen Toad? He doesn't do it any more, but he used to..."

"Stop." This was not happening. We were still on the porch and I had the rail in a death grip. "I don't understand. How the fuck is this not something you tell me?"

"What do you mean? I thought you knew. Emily knows. I thought she told you when she set the two of you up?"

That left me speechless. There were no words.

"Cody. It didn't mean anything. Seriously. Please don't…I can't take anymore. Every time I turn around, you're hating me." I watched him sit on the first step, shoulders hunched.

"Every time you turn around? Oh my god! First you're straight. You just want to know what *all the fuss is about*. Then, you tell me you love me. Then you tell Sophie you love her. Then you're gay and Sophie's known all along. And you've been with other guys. And now. And now one of those guys is Ashton. God, I'm so tired of this." I went inside, wiping tears from my eyes. "I just. I just don't know anymore. I was so…" Happy was the word that came to mind, but the very idea of saying it seemed ridiculous now.

"Beaumont. You have to believe me. The last thing I want to do is hurt you."

I laughed. "Why do people say that? Seriously, It's always I never meant to hurt you. It's never the truth: I didn't want to get hurt. It's I want to get what I want and if you get hurt, well *then* it's I never wanted to hurt you. This self preservation bullshit of yours is getting so fucking old."

"Cody."

"You know what. Do me a favor. When Ashton gets here, tell him to go fuck himself."

I closed the door and locked it, bereft of emotion, numb and cold. I slumped down as Aiden first knocked then banged on the door, calling my name.

CHAPTER TWENTY-THREE

Lost

I pulled over cursing, the FIAT skittering across the gravel on the shoulder. I turned off the radio. Red and blue lights lit up the interior. I looked in the rearview mirror and watched the officer sauntering towards me. I could almost hear the click-click-click of his ballpoint pen.

"License and registration." I rolled my eyes and reached into the glove compartment. "Do you know how fast you were going?"

"No sir." Which was the truth. I didn't care how fast I was going. Didn't care about anything really. All I wanted was to get away from everything. Everyone: Emily, Aiden, and Ashton.

"83 miles an hour." *Was that all?* "Mister...." He held my driver's license up into the beams of his flashlight. "Beaumont. Is there a reason you were driving so fast? Some emergency."

I shook my head. "No sir. I just didn't know how fast I was going."

"Where are you headed?"

"I don't know."

The officer drew the beam of his flashlight to my face, blinding me momentarily.

"Is everything okay, son?"

I shrugged my shoulders and stared into the beam of light. I didn't know. He turned the flashlight off and I blinked, bright after images like fireflies flashed behind my eyelids.

"Is something wrong?" The officer leaned down.

I shook my head again and stared straight ahead. My phone vibrated in my pocket.

"Have you been drinking?"

I wish. "No sir." My phone vibrated again: voicemail.

"I'll be right back."

I watched him in my rearview mirror again as he walked backwards a few steps behind my car. He turned the flashlight back on and played the beam off the telltale dents in my car.

A car drove over the ridge behind us and drew the police officer's shadow on the road ahead. I watched it grow and shrink then completely disappear as the car passed us. I heard him walking.

"Okay." He pulled the ticket off the pad and handed it to me along with my license. "I'm writing a citation for speeding. 83 in a 55. And another for no rearview mirror. The speeding ticket requires a response within 30 days. Do you have any questions?"

"No sir." I looked down at the box with the rearview mirror that was sitting in passenger seat. *Fucking Sophie.* I gripped the steering wheel and stared up at the roof of the car.

"Maybe you should head on home. You don't seem to be in any shape to be out driving. And take it slow."

I stared blankly back at him "Yeah. Okay." I waited until he was back in his car before I started the engine.

It took me another 20 miles before it occurred to me where I was going. I pulled into the driveway. The lights were off in the house but the porch light was on. The porch light was *always* on. I got out of the car and stood in the grass, staring at the dark house. Crickets and the tick-tick of the engine broke the silence of the night. I watched as the light in the kitchen came on. A strip of light brightened the window as she peeked through the blinds. A moment later and she was opening the front door.

"Cody? Cody?" She shielded her eyes from the porch light. "What...What are you doing here? It's 3:30 in the morning."

"I'm fine. Thank you for asking."

"Don't sass me. " She came out draped in a night robe and slippers and grabbed me, pulling me into a hug. "Okay, out with it. Who did it this time?"

"I don't know what you're..."

"Cody Beaumont. Ain't nobody knows you better'n me. Nobody." She draped an arm over my shoulder and shuffled me towards the front door. "You get your heart broken and you show up at my doorstep, every time. Ever since that Tony Beecher boy when you was in the fourth grade."

A Kiss Is Just a Kiss

Remembering Tony Beecher, was like remember popsicles and cotton candy and above-ground swimming pools and hotdogs with just ketchup and white bread, playing army with little green plastic soldiers in the backyard or reading comic books with flashlights under the covers. We were inseparable, did everything together; until his mother caught me giving him a kiss. The ugly things she said, the ugly hate I felt. I ran to my Grams' house, afraid my mother would react the same way. I hid there with my Grams, helping make oatmeal cookies. My mother came and I had my first lesson in unconditional love as they both held me as I cried, my Grams shushing me softly as she stroked my hair, my mother holding me so tight I could barely breathe.

She had already poured me a glass of milk and I nearly laughed as she pulled the cookie jar off the counter and set it on the table. She put two giant oatmeal cookies on a napkin in front of me.

Grams liked to make her coffee on the stove in an old fashioned percolator. She ignored the brand new Keurig on the counter and filled the pot with water, measuring out the Folgers.

"Can I have a cup?"

She nodded and pulled down two oversized mugs from the cabinet. "Course you *can?*"

I rolled my eyes. *"May I* have a cup?"

"Yes you may." She sat at the table and folded her hands on top of the placemat. "So." She took one of the cookies in front of me and broke it in half, taking a bite out of one piece. "Spill it."

I started from the beginning and spared none of the details. I'd learned early on that Grams loved the details. She listened intently; nodding occasionally and I could see her thinking, formulating a response even as I dove deeper and deeper into the tale.

She interrupted me once to pour us more coffee, adding a good bit of cream to mine. Then when I was finished she got up, went to the refrigerator and pulled out the carton of eggs and some bacon. She made toast in the oven. We ate silently. She was still thinking, I could tell. After she sopped up the last of the egg yolk with a corner bit of toast she looked up at me.

"I know this has been hard on you. It'd be hard on anyone. Love is a hard thing. And harder still when you're afraid. Afraid of bein' hurt. Afraid of bein' rejected." She reached across the breakfast table and took my hand. "You know how hard it was for you. How hard it is for *you*." I nodded. It was the only response I could muster, seeing the look in her eyes. "Now you just imagine. If you didn't have me. Or your mother. Who loves you no matter what? Those two boys are livin' in a world o' hurt. Sounds to me like they're afraid of everything. Everything but loving you."

Grams frowned. "Don't think I don't know how it feels. Your Grand was a hard man to live with. And he had his secrets. He was a good man and I loved him as best I could with as much as I could. I learned that some secrets are meant to be secrets. Some lies are meant to be told. The truth is s'pose to be an easy thing. But there are a few things you need to know about the truth. One, your truth and my truth are not the same and that goes for everyone. And truth always comes with time, you don't rush it.

Those two boys of yours are just like little Tony Beecher. You've gone and given them a kiss. You 'member what I tol' you about that." She nodded to herself, reaffirming her truth from so long ago. "A kiss is just a kiss. Ain't nothing wrong with that kiss. Ain't nothing wrong with givin' one. As long as you know that the truth behind that kiss is gonna be different for everyone."

Grams picked up my empty plate and hers and put them in the sink. She ran a little warm water over them and scrubbed them with a brush and a squirt of Palmolive. She rinsed them with more water and set them in the drainer.

"Grams, what should I do?"

"I don't know. I suspect you do though. It's just gonna take time to figure it out."

CHAPTER TWENTY-FOUR

No Matter What

I could smell the clove cigarettes before I opened the front door. The scent grew stronger as I entered my apartment.

"Ash?" I listened intently in the silence but heard nothing. I wondered if he was still here. There was a makeshift ashtray on the coffee table; a Dr. Pepper can torn in half, the aluminum curled and folded ornately. It held half a dozen cigarette butts. White ash had drifted and dotted the tabletop. His little black flask lay on its side, empty. I picked it up and smelled the familiar aroma of orange liqueur. I could almost taste that first kiss at Chloe's party.

I tried to think back, though it wasn't that difficult, to remember any telltale signs of who Ashton really was, but the only recollections planted firmly in my memory were more tactile, more physical in nature; his touch, his kiss, the first night in his bed.

It was easy to see how he *could* be a prostitute; my struggle was more *why* he would be. I had to keep reminding myself that he wasn't anymore.

Admittedly, I was scandalized. I wouldn't have told anyone either. Did that make me a hypocrite?

I walked back to my bedroom. Passing the bathroom, I noticed a black tank top and a pair of jeans puddled on the floor outside the shower stall, a towel draped over the frosted glass door. I walked in and picked up the clothes. I could smell Ashton, his sweet natural musk, his clove cigarettes and I flashed to the moment I saw him from under the eucalyptus tree with Emily as he blew smoke rings into the air. I left his clothes on the vanity and went into my bedroom.

Ashton slept in my bed. The dark blue sheets had been kicked away and were now tangled at his feet. All he wore was a pair of neon pink briefs with little dancing penguins. I was enchanted. I couldn't help but stare, my eyes drawn across his lithe form. I couldn't focus, my eyes leapt from his pouty lips to his legs, to his provocatively enticing bulge accentuated by the tiny pink briefs. His chest rose subtly as he slept and then, as if he felt my eyes on him, he turned on his side, away from me and towards the window. The morning light glowed on the contours of his hip, the slip of his waist, and the curve of his shoulder. I recalled the feel of that soft flesh and imagined slipping the briefs off of him. A shiver ran through me as I drank in this divine image. The memory of our first time, of him under me, and riding me, me deep inside of him, our bodies straining as we climaxed, dizzied me and left me breathless. . I lost myself in him. I backed out of the room and went back into the bathroom. I stared at myself in the mirror, my cheeks flush, my eyes dilated. I leaned over the sink and threw handful after handful of cold water on my face.

Ashton stood in the doorway when I looked up again. He propped his head on the doorframe, his eyes concentrating on my face in the mirror His smile was sleepy and welcoming, but there was a lost sadness that wrecked me. I watched as he reached out and ran a finger tentatively along my shoulder and down my arm. His smile blossomed slowly as if he realized I was real and not a dream and the tears clinging to his eyelashes broke any resolve I might have had holding. I pulled him to me and he cried, grabbing fistfuls of my shirt to pull me tighter against him. I felt utterly distraught, lost in his sobs, which clawed at my heart and soul. I was aware of the repetitive "I'm sorry" he cried into my neck, each one stabbing me. Worse still, the pleading "don't hate me." Both brought me to tears. I could only hold him tighter.

We stood like that, clinging to each other, for what seemed like an eternity. Slowly the tide of his tears ebbed and he dabbed his cheeks on my shoulder. His breathing grew calm and shallow and for a moment I thought he might have fallen asleep. I stood a little straighter and he tightened his grip around my waist.

"Come on." I slid a hand down his arm and took his hand. I drew him like a lost ship and he drifted behind me from the bathroom to my bed. "Lay down."

Ashton crawled across the bed to the far side and lay down, grabbing a pillow and hugging it to him. I followed. He sighed as I draped an arm over him, tracing my lips across the back of his neck. He tilted his head back and I could smell the cocoa scent of my shampoo. He pushed the pillow away and wrapped my arm tighter around him, pulling my hand up to his lips; he kissed my palm over and over. He fidgeted and adjusted and maneuvered until he was satisfied that he couldn't get any closer to me. He sighed again.

"You just walked away?" Ashton whispered.

I was lost for a response. I opened my mouth to reply but had nothing. I'd been unfair to both Ashton and Aiden. Especially Ashton.

"You want to know the details?" Ashton pulled my arm tighter again. His played his hand up and down the length of my arm.

I shook my head. I *did* want to know the details but didn't believe I deserved to know them.

Ashton turned over and faced me. His cheeks were still wet from crying and I thumbed away the tear tracks.

"I loved my mother, more than anything in the world. I think she knew I was gay before even I did. She would tuck me in at night when I was little and kiss my forehead and tell me she loved me, loved all of me, no matter what. When I told her..." Ashton smiled, his eyes far away. "...When I told her I was gay, she called me her little butterfly, finally coming out of my cocoon. She kissed my forehead, wiped away my tears and told me she loved me, all of me, no matter what. Then she told me to go mow the lawn." Ashton wiped at his eyes, his smile broken. "My father, on the other hand. I think he knew, no, I know he knew. My parents must have talked about it when I was little. One day, I was his pride and joy, his *son*." His emphasis on the word son resonated with all the glorious implications of a proud father. "The next day it was like I didn't exist. He stopped looking at me. He started drinking. I know I wasn't the reason, not the only reason anyway. He lost his job. My mother got sick. It was one thing after another." Ashton shrugged his shoulder. "And he started drinking." His voice trailed off and I could tell he was remembering things, his eyes dashed from side to side like he was seeing everything right here in front of me. "The doctors, they said it was cancer. My fa..." He cleared his throat, his eyes hardened, losing their luster. He stared straight ahead, right through me. "My father, he confronted me, said I killed her. That she died of a broken heart. That I shouldn't have told her."

I shook my head, speechless. I'd never encountered such hate and rejection.

"I ran away. I mean, I know he was sad. He loved my mother. But he hated me. Hated me for a long time. I couldn't stay, not without my mother." He was back in the present, the memories, just that now, memory. "Anyway. I was fourteen when my mom died. I was out on the street. I tried to go back home, but my dad, sold the house. I haven't seen him since her funeral." He wiped his tears angrily. "I don't know why I'm crying over him. He doesn't deserve it. I don't care. He probably threw all my stuff away. I had the best beanie Baby collection you ever saw. I think my mom liked 'em, but didn't want to seem like a kid so she bought 'em for me. I had hundreds. My favorite was the Princess Diana cuz that's what she looked like, my mom. There's this one picture of her, where she's got her arms wrapped around her knees in that white dress and her tiara and that pearl necklace, when I see that picture, I always have to do a double take." He was quiet, this time for a few minutes. He'd closed his eyes, and was smiling so sweetly and I wondered if he was with his mother then and she was telling him how much she loved him, no matter what. I closed my eyes too, thinking of my mother, who loved me unconditionally. And my Grams who possibly loved me even more.

"I wanted to tell you. But I've learned not to share myself. I had no intention of falling for you." His eyes were shining again. "You and Aiden. And I have so much shit. It's easier not to fall in love."

I started to reply. I felt he deserved something anything, but he pressed a couple of fingers to my lips and silenced me.

"Can we just lay here?" He turned back over and faced the window, rolling back against me. "I don't want you to say anything. I just want you to know, I'm falling in love with you."

CHAPTER TWENTY-FIVE

Cinderella Wore Birkenstocks

I called Emily first thing and told her to get her ass over to my apartment. After a little backpedalling and begging, she relented. I waited on the balcony, rocking back and forth, chain smoking and drinking Dr. Pepper, my headphones filled with the rhythmic bliss of Lady Gaga.

"I still can't believe you didn't tell me."

"I promised I wouldn't." Emily shrugged her shoulders. "Besides, you wouldn't want me to tell any of *your* secrets, would you? 'Specially if I promised not to."

"No but…" I whined.

"Alright then." Her tone was dismissive. I'm sure we've had this conversation before, but still, she was my best friend. No secrets. That's the rule, right? "What kind of best friend are you?"

"The good kind." She picked up my copy of Entertainment Weekly and proceeded to act as if the subject was closed.

"*The good kind.*" I mocked. Emily glared at me over the magazine "I would think, *this* was something that you could have shared."

Emily sighed putting the magazine in her lap. She looked like my mother right before she gave me a good and thorough scolding.

"Something like that wasn't my place to tell. Especially since it's in the past. *His* past. Not to mention. You would have treated him completely different. And I promised him. Promised! And for you to sit there and…"

"Okay. Okay. You don't have to make a big deal out of it." That was the wrong thing to say.

"A *big deal*? A big deal? You're the one…" Emily stood up, her eyes rounded, her fist clinched at her side. I scrambled back against the far end of the couch. She loomed over me. "Cody Aaron Beaumont!"

"Whoa. Whoa. Whoa….There's no need to middle name me."

She grabbed a pillow and began pummeling me. I shouldn't laugh in these situations. For some reason, it gets her all riled up. But I couldn't help myself. I tried to stifle the laughter, but to no avail. She only hit me harder.

"Feel better?" I asked as she dropped the pillow in my lap and went back to the magazine.

"No. I'm still mad."

I laughed but slapped a hand over my mouth when she looked to start up again. "Why are you mad?"

"You went to Grams without me."

"I didn't even know I was going till I was there. If it makes you feel any better, she did ask about you." I tried a smile for her and she sat up straighter.

"She did?" I swear the girl was bipolar. Her smile beamed.

"Uh huh." Grams had that affect on everybody. I wanted very much to bring Ashton and Aiden to meet her. Though I was a little apprehensive. Grams didn't have a filter; everything she knew about me was fair game. And she had incriminating photographs that always came out when I brought friends.

"What'd she say? What'd she say?"

I rolled my eyes. "She just asked how you were. Stuff like that."

"What'd you tell her?" I rolled my eyes. This was routine Emily.

"Oh my god. I told her you were donating your boobs to science."

"You did not!" She crossed arms across her ample bosom and scowled.

I couldn't help but laugh. "Well, why'd you ask? I told her you were fine." I shook my head.

"And?"

I hated that question. There were so many question crammed inside that one word.

"And what?"

"And what did she say about Ashton and Aiden?"

"What makes you think we talked about…"?

A Kiss Is Just a Kiss

Emily has an assortment of expressions that I pretty much knew without her saying a word. The one she was giving me now spoke volumes; asking me "just how stupid do you think I am?" I stared up at the ceiling and took a deep breath. "She didn't say anything. Nothing about what I should do. She was all about self-reliance and being there to support whatever choice I made." I said it in a whiny sing-songy voice. She liked to say, "It's not what you choose, it's what you do after you choose that's important." As if I knew what I was going to choose much less what I was going to do after I chose.

Emily sighed. "So? What *are* you gonna do?"

"God I hate that question." It felt like I'd been asking myself that question for an eternity.

"I need a drink."

"Yeah cuz that's solves many a crisis." Emily's eyebrow perked up. "Although…" She looked at her Minnie Mouse watch. "They do have an early happy hour at *Princess*."

"The lesbo bar?"

"Excuse me?"

I tightened my grip on the throw pillow and inched back. "What I meant to say was…. the bar frequented by lovely lesbians?"

"Yes. The bar." She grabbed her purse and stood up abruptly. "Come on ya little bigot."

"Hey!"

"Don't hey me. You are. You don't like lesbians."

I couldn't help but laugh. "It's not cuz they're lesbians. And I don't hate them. I just don't like 'em. I mean, women in general." I retreated. "You excluded, of course."

"Oh please, if you took all the women out of your life, you'd be…"

I paused on my way to the door and tapped my foot. "I'd be what?"

"Let's just go." She whirled around and hustled down the stairs.

"That's what I thought." I muttered to myself.

I eyed Carlo on my way down the stairs. I still hadn't gotten the mirror replaced and he looked rather pathetic. The scratches along the driver's side of the car looked scabrous in the light of day. I cringed, mourning my poor baby as I followed Emily to her VW.

I think every time I see her car there's something wrong with it. A half-empty roll of Duct tape lay in the passenger seat and I knew repairs were underway for some newfound vehicular malady. I held the roll up as I sat down and Emily nodded towards the rearview mirror. The mirror, while still attached to the windshield appeared to have fallen out of its frame. Silver tape encircled the outer frame of the glass and covered about a third of the reflective surface. I shook my head. "You know, I looked it up. After I got my ticket. Legally we're only required to have *two* rear viewing mirrors. That cop was a prick; giving me a ticket for not having that other rearview mirror." I toyed with the edge of the Duct tape pulling about two inches of tape free and wrapping my forefinger. "I mean he could have just given me the one for speeding. Now I have to go and contest the ticket." I sighed dramatically.

"Oh you sound so put upon."

"I *am*." I don't know why my voice went up three octaves. "The world is out to get me. I've told you before, Fate….she's a bitch and I might point out…a woman."

Emily slipped her ancient iPhone adapter into the cassette slot of her stereo and turned up the volume. "I'm done listening to you." Bruno Mars started singing *When I Was Your Man* and all I could do was sink back and glare at the stereo. Then P!NK was happy to point out that I wasn't broken, just bent and that I could love again, she just wanted a reason.

Princess was, as I pointed out correctly to Emily, a lesbian bar. Located on the top floor of a newly renovated multi-purpose commercial venture in the gayborhood, it twinkled and glowed like a tiara, even in the light of day. An Urban Outfitters, a Starbucks, a GAP and an independent LGBT bookstore occupied the first floor.

The developers had kept a freight elevator that went solely to the top floor, as if this Cinderella wore Birkenstocks instead of glass slippers. On weekends the elevator had an attendant, to corral the busy unruly masses, but Emily and I rode up alone this afternoon, a muted bass thumping through a speaker secured behind a cage. I inspected a chaotic mass of names and profanities and hearts scratched into the wood veneer. Apparently I wasn't the only one who loved penis, though finding it scratched on the inside of an elevator lifting me up to a lesbian bar seemed out of place. Maybe it was a straight girl's cry of rebellion or a gay boy's.

A Kiss Is Just a Kiss

The Princess was lit brightly, music subdued: nothing too raucous so early in the day. A trio of women drinking afternoon martinis and cosmos sat at the end of the bar, perched on red leather barstools. Another woman, who could easily rip me in half, looked up as we walked in, giving Emily the once over. I might as well have been an ashtray in a nonsmoking building. I knew there was a reason I didn't like lesbian bars.

I followed Emily's lead and sat on one of the barstools. Emily quashed any temptation to whirl around like a kid on a 3-ticket carnival ride as she gripped me by the shoulder and admonished me with a sternly worded "No." My shoulders slumped and then she asked the magic question. "What do you want?" I perked right up.

"Vodka Redbull." I chirped. I toyed with the bar napkin. The bartender...bartendress...I don't know what you call a female bartender, scowled at me as she raised my drink to put it on the napkin. I smiled apologetically and put it back down.

"Ahhhhhh." I was right. I did need a drink. The bartender poured it; heavy on vodka, light on Redbull, which was just fine by me. We were on our seconds and I had my elbows on the bar, my chin propped in my palm. I gave Emily a sidelong glance as she fished out the olive in her martini. "Do you think I could keep both of 'em?"

"Both of 'em? Both of what?" Then realization hit and her eyes rounded. "Oh no. Oh no." She shook her head, "Cody!" She stretched out the y in my name so long that the bartender looked up. Emily leaned in closer to me. "They're not puppies. You can't be serious."

I was rocking back and forth, moving side to side with the rhythm of the music. I was a pro at barstool dancing. Emily stilled me with a firm grip on my shoulder. "Cody. Focus." She shook her head again. "No. Just no."

"But. I can't choose. I keep thinking I can. I mean I think about Aiden and I'm like he's the one." I grabbed my bar napkin and twisted it tightly. "Then I think Ashton's the one." I untwisted the napkin and flattened it out on the bar. "He was at the apartment when I got home from Grams." I was staring at the video screens over the bar, staring but not seeing. "He told me everything. Told me he loved me."

"What'd you say?"

I shook my head. "He wouldn't let me say anything. Just wanted to lie there." I sighed. "And all I wanted to do was tell him. Over and over again. I fell asleep with it echoing in my head. Then he was gone when I got up this morning." I look at Emily. "Is it wrong that I feel cheated?"

Emily leaned in again, this time wrapping both her arms around me in a big hug.

The three women from the end of the bar passed behind us, laughing as they headed for the elevator. I watched them over Emily's shoulder. All three of them were beautiful, two blondes and a brunette, dressed business casual, armed with clutch purses and iPhones. Two had already put phones to their ears as they sank from view in the freight elevator.

CHAPTER TWENTY-SIX

Beneath His Beautiful

Ashton

I watched Cody sleeping as I left. I felt an almost gravitational pull to fall back into bed with him. I felt it in my gut as I stepped into my jeans and had actually taken a step closer to him as I pulled on my t-shirt. If I hadn't stubbed my toe on the doorframe and looked away, I'm certain this gravity would have won and pulled me in and I'd be wrapped in his arms again and the fear and anxiety, the uncertainty wouldn't be tearing me up.

Did he love me? He'd said as much or tried to; but all I *knew* was I loved him. This love caught me by surprise, not just his love, but mine as well. I didn't think or rather I didn't believe anyone would love me again.

I say *again*, only because I certainly can't discount the love of my mother, whose unconditional love saved my life even after she was gone. Her love made me relevant when no one else did. I suppose that says something about me, that my first idea of love is my mother loving me. I don't think I can remember anyone else.

I built my walls, fastidious and strong, letting no one in, bound and determined to keep my heart intact, to keep it safe. But it was lonely.

I held firmly to the doorframe, pulling myself tight against it, as if it were a doorway through the very walls I had built.

I had no one to blame but myself. And Ems. She had made it her crusade to draw us together. She had started weeks before I met him for the first time. Ems deduced immediately my membership in, as she put it, "the Skittles brigade." While I cringed at such a notion, as if we took to the streets armed with bags of fruit flavored candies to fight for our right to be, still Ems and I bonded almost immediately. I'd say she chipped away at the walls I'd built, but truth be told, she tunneled right under them, oblivious of their very presence. She was tenacious and while it was easy to see she and Cody were best friends, she befriended me and made room for me without reservation. She was fierce, ferociously protective of Cody and the fact that she granted me access to this inner sanctum spoke volumes. She practically choreographed my first meeting with Cody. And then the second at The Frozen Toad, when she *just showed up*. I could have kicked her.

I cast a final sidelong glance at Cody. The pillow I'd been sleeping on was now firmly in his grasp, one corner tucked under his chin. *That could be you.* I stared up at the ceiling, silently bickering with the taunting inner voice.

I pulled his front door closed and pressed my forehead against it, my eyes closed. *Go back. You're so close.* I shook my head and forced myself down the stairs. The morning was cold, the dawning sunlight, a mere gray ambient light behind a veil of threatening rain clouds.

The drive home was a miserable affair. I tried listening to the radio but apparently love was in the air, certainly it was *on* the air, every song an audible taunt of what I wanted so dearly. I didn't dare play any of my own playlist as my musical tastes tended towards the overemotional. I turned off the radio and rolled down the windows, listening to the wind whip through the car instead, the cold air numbing. I drove too fast, blared my horn and gave a few of my fellow motorist the finger. The traffic was light but I raced up on cars and whipped around them like I was at home playing *Gran Turismo*. I yelled at the top of my lungs as I sped down the freeway, my grip on the steering wheel white knuckled. The first raindrop hit the windshield in inaudible plops that raced up the glass with the wind. Then I plunged into a curtain of rain, as if the sky had opened up. The rain was jarring as it beat down, a disharmonious rhythm, like dropping pennies on glass and the world beyond the window became a brake-light red prism. I sped on blindly for a few more moments before slamming on my brakes. The Jetta hydro-planed. I fought the urge to hit the brakes, but unfortunately jerked the wheel. The car skidded left and then spun. I watched wide-eyed the crimson flash of brake lights and then as I spun the brighter flash of headlights. Red. White. Red. White. After several revolutions I gained control of the car and drove to the shoulder. I sat there, breathless, the car idling quietly, my heart beating wildly. I heard a car horn blaring and look left. A group of teenagers, all flipped me the bird, laughing. I responded with a bark of laughter of my own. I was one of *those people* racing to nowhere, driving with reckless abandon only to find myself on the side of the road as everyone passed me. I lit a clove, the spiced scent conquering the spring rain.

The rain slackened as I sat there and I watched in the rearview mirror as a black Mercedes pulled off the freeway behind me. An umbrella sprouted from the driver's side like a mushroom. The man stood tall under the umbrella's canopy, waiting for the traffic to pass before he traipsed through the rain and stopped by my door. He leaned down and looked in at me. I rolled the window down.

"I thought that was you." Drake Niequist grinned; his ice-blue eyes and smile beckoning. He was the epitome of charm and guile, an enchantment come to life, one that had drawn me, like a siren's song, into a life I regretted.

The rain was gone and a sword of sunlight pierced the clouds; a rift in heaven lit bright.

The first time I saw Drake Niequist he stood before a bank of candles, the golden candlelight playing across his sharp features as he held an unlit wick to the flame of another candle. Then he knelt, clasped his hands together and prayed; his lips moving, words inaudible. His eyes were open and looking straight ahead, but he knew I watched. I looked away and when I looked back he stared at me. I caught my breath. He glowed with the candlelight. He rose, lithe and sinewy, a jaguar clothed in Brooks Brothers, his eyes pinning me to where I sat.

Churches were the best places to sleep; a refuge from the elements, especially from the cold and rain. Summer wasn't so bad, nights out under the stars were a welcome respite from the hard sun, but winter proved refuge a necessity. This winter had been particularly harsh, much like my life.

I didn't believe too strongly in God; my mother dead, my father gone, no amount of prayer brought them back, but the warm scent of candles, sometimes hundreds of them, flickering haloed prayers, these vigils of hope left me wondering if He was still there.

I'd been rotating churches and found that I preferred the Catholic cathedral best. One of the oldest buildings in Fairweather, the church had many nooks and crannies along the nave, shadowed sanctuaries for sleep or to while away the day when winter paid a visit.

"It's been awhile." Drake mused over his cup.

The hydroplaning had resulted in a flat tire and Drake offered to call Triple A. He insisted we wait in his Mercedes. After triple A fixed the tire he persuaded me to have coffee.

"It's the least you could do. We can catch up."

Drake Niequist didn't *catch up.* I guess he could read the doubt in my eyes. I studied his features. I remember finding him attractive, but there seemed to be something otherworldly to him, something beguiling in his nature. His smile was warm and comforting, but predatory; his eyes an artic blue that missed nothing.

"I'm not trying to play you. No ulterior motive. Just a cup of coffee and talk." He held his hands up in surrender, smiling. "The past is the past."

I relented.

The man wore cologne like a fine suit, perfectly tailored for his purpose. Sitting this close to him was an olfactory seduction. I tried breathing through my mouth, but I found myself inhaling deeply; the scent hypnotic, an inaudible siren drawing me closer to the proverbial jagged cliff that was Drake Niequist. The waitress offered refills, tucking lose strands of auburn hair behind her ear.

"Are you hungry?" He stood tall in front of me, the scent of warm wax wafted and comingled with a scent so warm and welcoming, I found myself nodding before I knew it. "Come on. We'll get you something." He held a hand out, guiding me beside him and maneuvering me through the pews, his hand heavy on my

shoulder. I felt the heat of his presence on the back of my neck as if the heat of all those candles emanated off of him.

His car was black and sleek; it glistened like black oil reflecting the cold moonlight. He opened the door for me and I sank into the luxurious leather seat.   He dropped my overstuffed backpack behind his seat as he slid into the driver's side. He smiled over at me, the engine started with a purr and he drove through the night like a cat, stalking quietly.   He glanced occasionally at solitary figures walking alone down quiet streest or standing under the luminous streetlights.

The diner was small but served breakfast 24 hours a day according to the hand-painted scrawl on the big glass windows.   It smelled of bacon and my stomach growled loudly.

"Get whatever you want."   He smiled again as he drew his phone out of the inner pocket of his suit.   He frowned and his thumbs flashed a rapid response to a text.

I ate ravenously.   Bacon, scrambled eggs, toast, pancakes with butter pecan syrup, a glass of milk and orange juice. He ordered another side of bacon for himself and ate it slowly, watching me eat, smiling the entire time.   I sopped up the syrup with a corner of toast and groaned miserably as I ate the last bite.

"You have a place to stay?"

"I hear you've a place off of Majesty."   Drake said.   "Nice location. I guess you didn't do too badly for yourself."

I stared at him, unwilling to give any ground.   I'd seen this approach.   And his inference to my past, to what paid for everything I had, caused an unhealthy anger to simmer.

"I'm not keeping tabs on you, if that's what you're thinking." He glanced out the window at a family climbing out of a Landrover.   He paid special attention to the teenage boy who followed the rest of the family by several paces. The boy was just Drake's type, would serve his purpose. He looked so familiar, the vulnerability, the estrangement, given different circumstances, he was me.

"You can stay with me."   The man didn't look at me as he spoke; his attention remained on the road.

"No thank you." I had heard all the stories. My imagination got the better of me. The idea of being left for dead on the side of the road or in a dirty alley plagued me.

"There's no need for you to go back to the church. I'm just right here."

The condominiums had gone up in the last year, the granite and glass crown jewel that was the cornerstone of the renewal efforts of the city council. We rode the elevator up in silence. I felt terribly out of place and dirty, unwilling to touch the dark mahogany walls in the elevator for fear of smudging the lustrous surface. The halls were hushed with a plush carpet that absorbed our footsteps. We stopped in front of an ornate door, the suite number chipped granite. He unlocked and swung the door inward, gesturing for me to enter. A crystal chandelier illuminated the main room, but beyond that, the floor to ceiling windows revealed a canvas of starlight and city lights, a mural of lights that drew the eye.

"Make yourself comfortable. I'll be right back."

I stood for a moment staring out at the night. I heard his voice and turned but I was alone in the room. A bar ran the length of one wall and I traced my fingers across the black granite surface. Several crystal decanters stood sentry at the far end. I lifted one of the stoppers and smelled a rich orange. Another lifted stopper revealed a creamy buttery aroma. I went back to the orange tracing my finger across the square stopper

"Would you like to try it?" His voice shook me.

Startled, I pulled my finger back and shook my head. I'd never had anything to drink. Butterflies flew rampant in my gut.

"It's okay. I'm having one. We'll call it a nightcap. It'll help you relax." He stood next to a black leather sofa, a pile of blankets and a pillow in his hand. He placed them on a square black coffee table below the chandelier. He strode purposefully behind the bar and grabbed two glasses. I watched him pour with rapt attention. He offered me a glass. Everything smelled of orange.

I slammed my cup down on the table. Coffee sloshed across the table. Drake stood abruptly, staring down at his lap. Satisfied that he hadn't gotten wet, he sat back down. His smile was back. "You were always protective." He ran his napkin across the table, soaking up the spilled coffee. He folded it in half once and then again and dropped it in his plate. "All I did was take care of you."

I fought back the tears.

"Is that what you call it?" I was incredulous.

Drake smiled with resignation, but his eyes bore into me. "The first time is always…"

"*THAT* was not my first time!" A hushed pause filled the restaurant, no voices, just the clinking of silverware and dishes. I lowered my voice. "That was something completely different. You took, you stole…" I accused, wiping at my eyes.

"Ashton." His placating tone unnerved me. As if my memories were false that the downward spiral my life had taken after meeting Drake was my doing. I couldn't possibly lay all the blame at Drake's feet, but the burden was not mine alone to bear. "I never intended…"

I glared at him. "You knew *exactly* what you were doing. I was fourteen." I whispered the last, a sibilant appeal.

Drake leaned back in his seat, his silence giving voice to the truth.

"Here."

I smiled but tried to pull the glass away from the bottle. He'd refilled it once already. The room was spinning. The chandelier blurred, the stars and city lights beyond the window were fuzzy apparitions. The orange liqueur splashed partially into the glass but more ran across my fingers and onto the bar. He placed a couple of bar napkins on the spill and I watched transfixed as they drank the amber liquid. I reached for a napkin to wipe my hand but shifted sideways. Drake saved me from falling. I couldn't help but stare as he propped me back up and taking my hand he suckled the Grand Marnier from my fingers. The only other person to have sucked on my fingers was me, and it was nothing like this. I inhaled deeply, a stuttered inhalation like Morse code to my tightening gut. He had a hand on my waist, at first to keep me from falling off the stool but soon it traveled down my hip and he teased an erection, kneading my crotch and inner thigh. The novelty of someone else touching me was such that when he leaned in and kissed me the first time, I came with a guttural whimper, shuddering against him.

I wondered if he remembered, or if I was merely a notch on the proverbial bedpost. I don't know why I cared, why I felt I needed to have meant something to him. Admittedly, I loved him, in some perverse way. He gave me a home, provided all the necessities of life and in my narrow view of 14 years of life, at the time, I thought he loved me too. His seduction had been complete. His words, and to a greater extent, his touch had been the balm to an unmoored broken soul, drifting about aimlessly.

"Here," He reached for the bill. "Let me get that."

I snatched it off the table. I held it to my chest, guarding it against his reach.

"Ashton. Please. It's just coffee." He shook his head, as if everything else I had, my home, my car, weren't paid for by him, negating the very notion that what *I* had done helped pay for everything *he* had.

He'd done this before: standard operating procedure. His smile, his voice, his eyes; I wanted to scream, to rage against the charming façade. If I could strike him, just once, I would. But once would never be enough. One would lead to two then three. I wouldn't be able to stop.

He pulled out his wallet and flipped through the bills, pulled free a twenty and dropped it on the table. "It's nothing."

You were nothing.

I swallowed, angry. Angry that he didn't have to say it, that the thought came so freely. Angry that the tears I fought were for myself.

I flew from the table, throwing the wadded check.

The air was cool outside the restaurant. There was no hint that it had rained. The wind blew softly, the sky was a freshly scrubbed blue and the sun shone brightly. I knocked a cigarette from the pack and leaned against the brick wall of the restaurant, next to a smoker's pole. My hands shook so badly, it took three tries to light my cigarette. I smoked angrily, blowing the smoke in great audible plumes. I slammed the flat of my shoe against the brick wall, listening to the rubber slap of the sole, again and again until my foot tingled. I did scream then, until my throat hurt. I flung the smoker's pole across into the parking lot. The base came free as it made contact with the asphalt. The metallic clang and a plume of ash drifted on the breeze. Hundreds of cigarette butts bounced like popcorn. I caught a glimpse of Drake's car. I shook the thoughts of destruction from my head.

I pulled out my phone.
"I need you."
"Where are you?"
I told him.

I paced in front of the restaurant, glimpsed Drake through the window. He had cornered the teen from earlier.

I couldn't hear what Drake said, but I didn't need to hear it. I saw the look in the boy's eyes. Drake must have caught him on the way back from the restroom. There was apprehension but an undeniable interest shone brightly as well. Drake leaned into the boy's personal space. Drake laughed at something the boy said, and then noticed me. His eyes sparkled and he winked at me.

I staggered away from the window as if struck. I stumbled over the smoker's pole. The pole rolled a few feet and came to a stop under the tire of Drake's car. I looked down at it then turned back and watched Drake. He still watched me.

The look in his eyes was priceless as I picked up the metallic pole. It was cold in my grip; the air pungent with the smell of stale cigarette smoke and tobacco.

The first swing knocked the Mercedes hood emblem from its grommet. It flipped through the air catching the sunlight like a tossed coin: heads or tails. I grinned and swung the pole again and again.

Someone yelled my name.

Cody stared at me through his passenger window. "Come on."

I leaned down and picked up the Mercedes emblem and put it in my pocket. Cody leaned across and pushed open the passenger door. I stood up and noticed Drake. He spoke with a great deal of agitation into his phone.

Sitting in Cody's car, I looked over at him as his tires squealed and we rocketed away from the restaurant. I sighed. "God, I've missed you."

Cody smirked, his eyes shining. "I saw you this morning."

I looked down at my hands and smiled. "I know, but it feels like a lifetime."

The first time I saw Drake Niequist he stood before a bank of candles, the golden candlelight playing across his sharp features as he held an unlit wick to the flame of another candle. Then he knelt, clasped his hands together and prayed; his lips moving, words inaudible. His eyes were open and looking straight ahead, but he knew I watched. I looked away and when I looked back he stared at me. I caught my breath. He glowed with the candlelight. He rose, lithe and sinewy, a jaguar clothed in Brooks Brothers, his eyes pinning me to where I sat.

Churches were the best places to sleep; a refuge from the elements, especially from the cold and rain. Summer wasn't so bad, nights out under the stars were a welcome respite from the hard sun, but winter proved refuge a necessity. This winter had been particularly harsh, much like my life.

I didn't believe too strongly in God; my mother dead, my father gone, no amount of prayer brought them back, but the warm scent of candles, sometimes hundreds of them, flickering haloed prayers, these vigils of hope left me wondering if He was still there.

I'd been rotating churches and found that I preferred the Catholic cathedral best. One of the oldest buildings in Fairweather, the church had many nooks and crannies along the nave, shadowed sanctuaries for sleep or to while away the day when winter paid a visit.

"It's been awhile." Drake mused over his cup.

The hydroplaning had resulted in a flat tire and Drake offered to call Triple A. He insisted we wait in his Mercedes. After triple A fixed the tire he persuaded me to have coffee.

"It's the least you could do. We can catch up."

Drake Niequist didn't *catch up.* I guess he could read the doubt in my eyes. I studied his features. I remember finding him attractive, but there seemed to be something otherworldly to him, something beguiling in his nature. His smile was warm and comforting, but predatory; his eyes an artic blue that missed nothing.

"I'm not trying to play you. No ulterior motive. Just a cup of coffee and talk." He held his hands up in surrender, smiling. "The past is the past."

I relented.

The man wore cologne like a fine suit, perfectly tailored for his purpose. Sitting this close to him was an olfactory seduction. I tried breathing through my mouth, but I found myself inhaling deeply; the scent hypnotic, an inaudible siren drawing me closer to the proverbial jagged cliff that was Drake Niequist. The waitress offered refills, tucking lose strands of auburn hair behind her ear.

"Are you hungry?" He stood tall in front of me, the scent of warm wax wafted and comingled with a scent so warm and welcoming, I found myself nodding before I knew it. "Come on. We'll get you something." He held a hand out, guiding me beside him and maneuvering me through the pews, his hand heavy on my shoulder. I felt the heat of his presence on the back of my neck as if the heat of all those candles emanated off of him.

His car was black and sleek; it glistened like black oil reflecting the cold moonlight. He opened the door for me and I sank into the luxurious leather seat. He dropped my overstuffed backpack behind his seat as he slid into the driver's side. He smiled over at me, the engine started with a purr and he drove through the night like a cat, stalking quietly. He glanced occasionally at solitary figures walking alone down quiet streest or standing under the luminous streetlights.

The diner was small but served breakfast 24 hours a day according to the hand-painted scrawl on the big glass windows. It smelled of bacon and my stomach growled loudly.

"Get whatever you want." He smiled again as he drew his phone out of the inner pocket of his suit. He frowned and his thumbs flashed a rapid response to a text.

I ate ravenously. Bacon, scrambled eggs, toast, pancakes with butter pecan syrup, a glass of milk and orange juice. He ordered another side of bacon for himself and ate it slowly, watching me eat, smiling the entire time. I sopped up the syrup with a corner of toast and groaned miserably as I ate the last bite.

"You have a place to stay?"

"I hear you've a place off of Majesty." Drake said. "Nice location. I guess you didn't do too badly for yourself."

I stared at him, unwilling to give any ground. I'd seen this approach. And his inference to my past, to what paid for everything I had, caused an unhealthy anger to simmer.

"I'm not keeping tabs on you, if that's what you're thinking." He glanced out the window at a family climbing out of a Landrover. He paid special attention to the teenage boy who followed the rest of the family by several paces. The boy was just Drake's type, would serve his purpose. He looked so familiar, the vulnerability, the estrangement, given different circumstances, he was me.

"You can stay with me." The man didn't look at me as he spoke; his attention remained on the road.

"No thank you." I had heard all the stories. My imagination got the better of me. The idea of being left for dead on the side of the road or in a dirty alley plagued me.

"There's no need for you to go back to the church. I'm just right here."

The condominiums had gone up in the last year, the granite and glass crown jewel that was the cornerstone of the renewal efforts of the city council. We rode the elevator up in silence. I felt terribly out of place and dirty, unwilling to touch the dark mahogany walls in the elevator for fear of smudging the lustrous surface. The halls were hushed with a plush carpet that absorbed our footsteps. We stopped in front of an ornate door, the suite number chipped granite. He unlocked and swung the door inward, gesturing for me to enter. A crystal chandelier illuminated the main room, but beyond that, the floor to ceiling windows revealed a canvas of starlight and city lights, a mural of lights that drew the eye.

"Make yourself comfortable. I'll be right back."

I stood for a moment staring out at the night. I heard his voice and turned but I was alone in the room. A bar ran the length of one wall and I traced my fingers across the black granite surface. Several crystal decanters stood sentry at the far end. I lifted one of the stoppers and smelled a rich orange. Another lifted stopper *revealed a creamy buttery aroma. I went back to the orange tracing my finger across the square stopper*

"Would you like to try it?" His voice shook me.

Startled, I pulled my finger back and shook my head. I'd never had anything to drink. Butterflies flew rampant in my gut.

"It's okay. I'm having one. We'll call it a nightcap. It'll help you relax." He stood next to a black leather sofa, a pile of blankets and a pillow in his hand. He placed them on a square black coffee table below the chandelier. He strode purposefully behind the bar and grabbed two glasses. I watched him pour with rapt attention. He offered me a glass. Everything smelled of orange.

I slammed my cup down on the table. Coffee sloshed across the table. Drake stood abruptly, staring down at his lap. Satisfied that he hadn't gotten wet, he sat back down. His smile was back. "You were always protective." He ran his napkin across the table, soaking up the spilled coffee. He folded it in half once and then again and dropped it in his plate. "All I did was take care of you."

I fought back the tears.

"Is that what you call it?" I was incredulous.

Drake smiled with resignation, but his eyes bore into me. "The first time is always…"

"*THAT* was not my first time!" A hushed pause filled the restaurant, no voices, just the clinking of silverware and dishes. I lowered my voice. "That was something completely different. You took, you stole…" I accused, wiping at my eyes.

"Ashton." His placating tone unnerved me. As if my memories were false that the downward spiral my life had taken after meeting Drake was my doing. I couldn't possibly lay all the blame at Drake's feet, but the burden was not mine alone to bear. "I never intended…"

I glared at him. "You knew *exactly* what you were doing. I was fourteen." I whispered the last, a sibilant appeal.

Drake leaned back in his seat, his silence giving voice to the truth.

"Here."

I smiled but tried to pull the glass away from the bottle. He'd refilled it once already. The room was spinning. The chandelier blurred, the stars and city lights beyond the window were fuzzy apparitions. The orange liqueur splashed partially into the glass but more ran across my fingers and onto the bar. He placed a couple of bar napkins on the spill and I watched transfixed as they drank the amber liquid. I reached for a napkin to wipe my hand but shifted sideways. Drake saved me from falling. I couldn't help but stare as he propped me back up and taking my hand he suckled the Grand Marnier from my fingers. The only other person to have sucked on my fingers was me, and it was nothing like this. I inhaled deeply, a stuttered inhalation like Morse code to my tightening gut. He had a hand on my waist, at first to keep me from falling off the stool but soon it traveled down my hip and he teased an erection, kneading my crotch and inner thigh. The novelty of someone else touching me was such that when he leaned in and kissed me the first time, I came with a guttural whimper, shuddering against him.

I wondered if he remembered, or if I was merely a notch on the proverbial bedpost. I don't know why I cared, why I felt I needed to have meant something to him. Admittedly, I loved him, in some perverse way. He gave me a home, provided all the necessities of life and in my narrow view of 14 years of life, at the time, I thought he loved me too. His seduction had been complete. His words, and to a greater extent, his touch had been the balm to an unmoored broken soul, drifting about aimlessly.

"Here," He reached for the bill. "Let me get that."

I snatched it off the table. I held it to my chest, guarding it against his reach.

"Ashton. Please. It's just coffee." He shook his head, as if everything else I had, my home, my car, weren't paid for by him, negating the very notion that what *I* had done helped pay for everything *he* had.

He'd done this before: standard operating procedure. His smile, his voice, his eyes; I wanted to scream, to rage against the charming façade. If I could strike him, just once, I would. But once would never be enough. One would lead to two then three. I wouldn't be able to stop.

He pulled out his wallet and flipped through the bills, pulled free a twenty and dropped it on the table. "It's nothing."

You were nothing.

I swallowed, angry. Angry that he didn't have to say it, that the thought came so freely. Angry that the tears I fought were for myself.

I flew from the table, throwing the wadded check.

The air was cool outside the restaurant. There was no hint that it had rained. The wind blew softly, the sky was a freshly scrubbed blue and the sun shone brightly. I knocked a cigarette from the pack and leaned against the brick wall of the restaurant, next to a smoker's pole. My hands shook so badly, it took three tries to light my cigarette. I smoked angrily, blowing the smoke in great audible plumes. I slammed the flat of my shoe against the brick wall, listening to the rubber slap of the sole, again and again until my foot tingled. I did scream then, until my throat hurt. I flung the smoker's pole across into the parking lot. The base came free as it made contact with the asphalt. The metallic clang and a plume of ash drifted on the breeze. Hundreds of cigarette butts bounced like popcorn. I caught a glimpse of Drake's car. I shook the thoughts of destruction from my head.

I pulled out my phone.
"I need you."
"Where are you?"
I told him.

I paced in front of the restaurant, glimpsed Drake through the window. He had cornered the teen from earlier.

I couldn't hear what Drake said, but I didn't need to hear it. I saw the look in the boy's eyes. Drake must have caught him on the way back from the restroom. There was apprehension but an undeniable interest shone brightly as well. Drake leaned into the boy's personal space. Drake laughed at something the boy said, and then noticed me. His eyes sparkled and he winked at me.

I staggered away from the window as if struck. I stumbled over the smoker's pole. The pole rolled a few feet and came to a stop under the tire of Drake's car. I looked down at it then turned back and watched Drake. He still watched me.

The look in his eyes was priceless as I picked up the metallic pole. It was cold in my grip; the air pungent with the smell of stale cigarette smoke and tobacco.

The first swing knocked the Mercedes hood emblem from its grommet. It flipped through the air catching the sunlight like a tossed coin: heads or tails. I grinned and swung the pole again and again.

Someone yelled my name.

Cody stared at me through his passenger window. "Come on."

I leaned down and picked up the Mercedes emblem and put it in my pocket. Cody leaned across and pushed open the passenger door. I stood up and noticed Drake. He spoke with a great deal of agitation into his phone.

Sitting in Cody's car, I looked over at him as his tires squealed and we rocketed away from the restaurant. I sighed. "God, I've missed you."

Cody smirked, his eyes shining. "I saw you this morning."

I looked down at my hands and smiled. "I know, but it feels like a lifetime."

CHAPTER TWENTY-SEVEN

Homecoming

Cody

"You wanna tell me what that was all about?" I tried to keep my eyes on the road, but the sun reflected in the streaks running down his cheeks. "You were beating the shit out of that Beemer."

"I need a place to stay." Ashton stared straight ahead.

"What?" I merged onto the freeway. "What do you mean a place to stay?"

I can't…" I watched his throat working, swallowing; tears, pride, pain.

"What about your place?"

"…Stay there anymore." He continued, leaning against the passenger window and staring up at the sky. "It's not really mine."

I guess I knew what he was saying. I wasn't about to make him spell it out. The truth was it didn't matter anymore. "You can't stay with me. I don't want you to stay with me." I kept glancing over at him, watched him close his eyes and nod to himself. Looking straight ahead, watching the traffic, I reached blindly for his hand. "Ashton, I don't want you to *stay* with me, I want you to *live* with me." Did I just say that?

"Thank you." His whisper was sibilant under the staccato intake of breath. He squeezed my hand. "For the record…" He smiled tentatively. He still hadn't looked over at me, but that little smile quieted the sudden storm inside my head. He let go of my hand to wipe his cheeks. He turned the rearview mirror and gasped at his reflection. "…You're crazy."

"As Grams likes to say, you're preaching to the choir and they done heard this sermon." I turned the mirror back so I could see behind me. "And quit that. You look fine." I flipped the shade down in front of him so he could use the mirror there instead. He leaned forward to get a better look and rubbed at his eyes.

"You're biased." He accused, his voice muted behind hands rubbing color back into his cheeks.

"Only a little."

This time he laughed.

"Soooooo…are you okay?"

Ashton nodded again. "I'm fine. I just…" He pulled a leg up under him. "Do you believe everything happens for a reason?"

"What do you mean?"

Ashton shrugged. "I guess I just never thought I'd be here, like this"

"Like this? What's that supposed to mean? Oh my God. You're not gonna tell me you're damaged goods or something stupid like that?"

"Well I am!" He turned back towards the window, pouting.

"Ashton. Ashton, look at me. You're no more damaged than anyone else."

He shook his head. "Not you. You're practically perfect."

I grinned shaking my own head in response.

"What?" He asked.

"Nothing. It's just, that's what I told Emily about you."

"Huh? Me. I'm not perfect. I'm fucked up." I laughed at him.

"Cody, I'm serious. You didn't even know about me; about the things I've done."

"I don't care."

"Bullshit."

"Okay, fine, you're right. I did care. I do care. But…. you can't change what happened. You can't change the past. I can't change it. It's over. We're gonna make the best of things. You're not that person anymore. And the Ashton *I know* was never that guy."

"It's part of me." His sigh filled the car.

"Ash. You can't do that."

"You can't tell me what I can or cannot do." The anger and frustration in his voice was subdued. "You don't know. You have no idea…"

"So fucking tell me already! You kept it a secret so I wouldn't know. Well now I know. It's not a secret anymore. Tell me and quit holding it against me that my life didn't suck as much as yours." I focused on the rearview mirrors, adjusting them needlessly and then fiddled with the stereo volume. I cast a subtle glance over at Ashton and he watched me with a quirky grin.

"You know, if I didn't know any better, I'd think you were still a little pissed." Ashton chided.

"Well..."

"Oh my gosh. I know what it is. You're jealous. You're jealous that I slept with Aiden before you did."

"The car swerved as I jerked the wheel in response. "I'm not jealous! I... Where the hell did that come from? You... He... I mean.... why would I be.... how could I be jealous?" The truth was I wasn't jealous...At least I didn't think I was. Not until he said it out loud. And I didn't know if I was more jealous of Aiden or Ashton. I remembered waking and seeing Aiden's hand on Ashton's thigh. I really didn't know what the hell I was doing.

"So what'd you think?" Ashton had turned in his seat again and was staring at me. The smile on his face was priceless.

"What'd I think? About what?"

"Aiden."

"I'm not telling you." I don't know why I was suddenly feeling territorial and secretive.

"I like his dick." He said while playing with a loose lock of hair.

I was speechless. My mouth was working but nothing was coming out.

Ashton laughed. "And his butt. D'you notice how perfect his butt cheeks are. I mean, they're like perfectly round."

"Hey!" I couldn't believe we were talking about Aiden. Okay, technically *we* weren't.

"What? I'm just sayin'. I had to bite them. One for each cheek." His voice was sing-song nonchalance.

I didn't mean to reach over and hit him, but I did. It was an innocent whack on the arm but... *Aiden was mine.*

"You don't want to share?" Ashton pouted, rubbing his arm.

"Share? He's not a toy. Why... why are we even having this conversation?"

His grin was back. "I thought it was more interesting than the first one."

We'd made it off the freeway alive and were sitting at the red light down the street from my apartment. I looked over at him and shook my head. In the last ten minutes we'd had pretty much 5 different conversations. I was starting to feel a little bipolar. "We're not done talking. Just so you know."

Ashton nodded then looked straight ahead. "Good." He took a deep breath. "So can I still stay…live with you?"

"I would like nothing better." My response was stilted. I was still a little pissed about the whole Aiden stuff. I don't know why. Did I have a right to be jealous? How many times had I pushed Aiden away while embracing Ashton? Sure, Aiden and I were fine now, better than fine, but I had a feeling, now that Ashton was going to be living with me, things were going to change again.

CHAPTER TWENTY-EIGHT

A Splash of Cold Reality

Ashton stared at me over the top of the car as I got out. He had that look: *don't look now but the shits about to hit the fan.* I glanced over my shoulder and I have to admit I expected a half-crazed blonde girl armed with a baseball bat. Ashton cleared his throat and I looked back at him. He jerked his head up and to the right a little: *up there you idiot.* I tried to ignore the sudden boom-boom-boom in my heart, like I'd been caught red-handed doing something wrong.

Aiden sat on my balcony. He was drinking a Coke and smoking. I gave him a tentative smile. He responded by getting up and walking into the apartment.

"This is gonna be fun." Ashton turned around and leaned against the car door and knocked a cigarette from the pack. "I'll wait here. Until you smooth the way."

"Oh no you don't." I rounded the back end of the car and grabbed his cigarette and took a nice long pull before crushing it out on the asphalt. "This was your idea."

"Yeah but he looked mad."

I laughed. "Thank you captain obvious." I grabbed his hand. "Come on, let's get this over with."

Ashton whimpered.

"Oh quit it. What's the worst that could happen? I mean the last time the two of you got in a fight…"

"You got knocked unconscious, cut the hell out of your foot and look!" Ashton pointed to a tiny scar above his lip. "I'm scarred forever!"

I paused a moment and pulled Ashton into a kiss. "My hero."

Ashton pulled back and looked at my face.

"What? I'm being serious. You fought for me. It's your battle scar." I leaned in to kiss him again.

Ashton shoved me. "Oh shut up." He was smiling as he started for the stairs. "This is why you're so much trouble. You say things like that."

"What?" I tried sounding innocent, but Aston was having none of it.

"Don't what me." He stopped at the foot of the stairs, glancing back at me. "You know it's true."

I shrugged my shoulders. "I'm cute. I can't help it."

"Aiden's not gonna have the chance to kick your ass, I'm gonna do it."

I couldn't help but laugh. I elbowed him as I raced past and up the stairs. "Wait your turn."

I opened the door, tentatively peering in and jumped as Ashton pressed up against me from behind.

"Fucker!" I whispered. "You scared me."

"What, you knew I was behind you, asstard." He shoved me further into my apartment, gathering me up in his arms as he did so, his reluctance gone. His hands stayed on my hips as Aiden came out of the bathroom.

"Hey." Aiden dropped down onto the couch and stared up at the both of us.

"Hey." Ashton and I responded simultaneously, Ashton's response echoing in my ear.

"So." I stepped out of Ashton's comfortable warm embrace. "I guess I should tell you." I looked back at Ashton for moral support.

"Tell me what?"

"Ashton and I…"

"I'm going to be staying here." Ashton finished.

Aiden looked at me, then at Ashton then back at me again, an eyebrow raised.

"So that's it then?"

"What…what's it?" I looked back at Ashton and he had a satisfied grin. I whacked him in the chest. I turned back to Aiden. "Aiden, we're not…" *Shit.* "I mean, he's just…" *Shit shit.* I knew if I turned around I'd see Ashton with his arms crossed and a curious smile across his lips.

"So you're gonna pick the *whore* over me?" He flung the words.

"He's not a whore!" I said but Ashton deflected the question with one of his own.

"You're gonna pick the lying asshole prick who's too chicken shit to admit he's a fag?" His words were calm and found their mark.

Ashton pushed around me and stood face to face with Aiden. Their chests bumped and both had fists bunched

"Ah fuck." It came out as an exaggerated sigh. "You're kidding, right?" I maneuver myself between them. It wasn't lost on me what happened the last time I tried to get in between them. "Look. I love you guys." They were bumping chests or trying to but squishing me instead. "Would you guys stop!"

"Tell him to stop."

I don't know which one said it as they jostled and manhandled me out of the way. Clearly there was something wrong with me. I was a little excited. I could almost taste the testosterone and the air was filled with a dizzying scent. "Guys." They both shrugged my hand off as I tried to separate them again. "Seriously, guys. I mean it." Aiden shoved Ashton. Ashton wasn't nearly as tall as Aiden, or as built but he shoved him back all the same, putting his whole body into it, the momentum carrying him up on his toes. "Guys?" I suddenly felt invisible. I had learned my lesson though. I stepped back and watched their posturing and shoving. They were so close they could have kissed. It was easy to imagine. Their cheeks were flush. I might as well have been on another planet. They circled one another like two feral animals. All that was missing was the growling and claws. "Guys?"

It wasn't difficult to tear myself away unseen. I went to the kitchen and grabbed the biggest glass I had, which happened to be a plastic Big Gulp cup from 7 Eleven. I filled it with water, humming to myself. I watched as they continued to tussle with one another. It was still hot to watch and I had to adjust myself in my shorts as I waited for the cup to fill up. It takes a lot longer without ice, but the water from the faucet comes out really cold.

I walked back into the living room. This had gone on long enough. Most of the water hit Aiden, a great deal of it splashing off his shoulder and catching Ashton in the face. I startled them, their reaction comical, almost cartoonish as they jumped. Two pair of eyes turned towards me.

"Hi. Remember me?" I reached back and grabbed my t-shirt and pulled it over my head. "I'm sure you two have a few things to *discuss.*"   I hooked a finger under the waistband of my basketball shorts hooking my briefs as well and tugged them down. "But, I was thinking." I stepped out of the shorts. Both Aiden and Ashton were oblivious of each other as they stared at my erection. "Maybe... just maybe, we could fast forward past destroying my apartment again."   It was easier to walk between them this time. Fingers glanced off of me and I felt Aiden lean towards me as I walk by him and towards my room. I turned back to them. "When you're through, I'll be in here."

CHAPTER TWENTY-NINE

That Sibilant Whisper

I crawled across my bed, wiggling my ass seductively in the air, *certain* they were shoving each other out of the way for first crack…. so to speak. I looked over my shoulder but the doorway was empty. I plopped down on the bed, fluffed my pillow and posed on my elbows, my erection pointing straight up in the air. I gave it a few tugs, you know, to keep the motor running, until my toes curled. I kept my eyes on the door and then it occurred to me: I was actually *waiting*. Don't get me wrong; it was flattering that they were fighting over me. Flattering as hell, but here I was, naked as the day I was born and much more of me to be naked, *and* stiff as a board. What's a boy got to do to get laid around here? I cleared my throat, my stare transforming into a glare as I waited. I listened for the telltale sounds of destruction; breaking furniture, tumbling bodies, but heard nothing. Then, I heard a muffled moan. *That* didn't sound like fighting, *at all*. I listened more intently. A muffled groan that sounded way too familiar had me climbing out of bed and inching slowly towards the door. I leaned against the doorframe my back pressed against the wall as I listened. I didn't want to admit what I was listening to; just as I didn't want to acknowledge the sudden excitement from the peanut gallery below. I looked down at my dick "Stop that!"

Then my memory decided to get into the act by flashing the image of waking up and seeing Ashton's hand resting on Aiden's bare hip after our little free for all.

Was there something more there?

I shook my head. I couldn't believe I was thinking that they were …well anything. Surely not. Another moan passed someone lips and I gripped the doorframe, torn between storming in there and throwing another glass of water at them or throwing myself at them.

My phone rang. It was on my bed and I dove for it. I landed painfully.

"Hello" My greeting came out weakly. "I think I broke my dick."

"TMI TMI TMI!" Em squealed in the phone. "What'd you do?"

"I was listening to Ashton and Aiden, in the living room. And..."

They're both there?"

"Well Ashton...had a thing.... and I had to go pick him up. And..."

"A thing?"

"Yes, a thing. And when we got home Aiden was already here. On my balcony. Waiting. And..."

"You're not going to tell me what Ashton's thing was?"

"No."

"Why cooooome?" Her voice was whiny and she thought she was being cute asking that way, but I wasn't falling for it.

"Oh don't even start. *You* kept his secret. So I..."

"It's a secret. Now you really have to tell me." I could imagine her jumping up on her knees, probably on her bed, a hungry expression on her face. "Just give me a hint."

"I'm not going to give you any hi...wait..." I paused, certain I heard someone say 'harder' from the living room. I listened. I looked at the wall, almost wishing I had X-ray vision."

"....Cody! Cody!"

"I think they're having sex in my living room." I got up and actually pressed my ear to the wall.

"Whaaaaaaaaaaat?!" I swear the girl could talk louder than anybody I knew. I pressed my phone against my chest while shushing her needlessly. I held my breath, listening.

Some dog started barking. It was the neighbor's stupid little yappy Chihuahua. If ever a dog needed a swift kick, it was that one. I rolled my eyes and glared in the direction of the offending bark.

"Emily. Emily. Did you call for a reason?" It sounded like she was hyperventilating. "Em!"

"I'm coming over." I could hear the determination in her voice.

"What! Why?" I took two steps towards the door and then two steps towards my bed then two steps towards the door again, torn as to what I was going to do. "No. You don't have to come over. I can handle this."

"Aiden's cheating on you. In your own living room!" Now there was a little anger in her voice. "I'm so going to…"

"Em. Em. I don't even know what's going on. How come you want to blame Aiden. I mean I just Ashton's moving in so…."

"What!? Ashton's moving in?"

"Yeeeeessssss?" I don't know why I was suddenly hesitant. I wanted Ashton with me

"And now they're having *sex* in your living room." She practically screamed the word sex.

"They're not having sex in my living room!"

The yapping Chihuahua had stopped its yapping. And the apartment was unnaturally quiet. Suddenly, it was like I was in one of those horror movies where you're terrified to look, but you know you *have* to. I turned to look at the door. Ashton and Aiden stood bare shoulder to bare shoulder just beyond the door to my bedroom.

Their jeans were unclasped, zippers down. It was obvious that Ashton had just pulled up his jeans; because his tight little briefs poked out or rather he didn't take the time to stuff himself back down. Aiden was going commando, naturally and I could tell he was swollen though not hard, still the view of the both of them was enticing. They both wore mischievous grins.

I'd forgotten I was talking to Emily until she was rambling on not so quietly on the other end.

"Em, I gotta go. Do *not* come over."

I let my phone slip from my grasp as I walked towards them.

"That was Em. She was going to come over and kick your ass, Aiden. *She* thought you were having sex with Ashton."

"Uh huh. She did, did she?" Aiden reached out to me, his fingers grasping.

I nodded stupidly.

I felt Ashton's lips on my neck, kissing softly, my neck, my jawline, then just under my ear. He bit my ear gently, then his tongue played along the lobe.

I could barely nod in response.

Aiden had grabbed me and sent familiar tremors rolling through me. I was up on my toes, my hips thrusting, while at the same time

Ashton's teeth bit at my neck. I was torn and quivering from their attention.

Ashton's whisper was sibilant and enthralling. "Aiden and I have come to an understanding."

CHAPTER THIRTY

Coming to an Understanding

"Didn't I tell you not to come over?" There was a pleading exasperation in my voice. I rubbed my face, letting the cool morning air wake me. "Just go ho…"

"I waited…"

"It's 6 in the fucking morning Em!" My frustration was getting the better of me. But I knew why she was here and was in no mood.

I cracked open the door a little, just enough to peek my head out where Emily stood on the porch. She'd been banging on the door for a good 10 minutes, yelling for me to open up. I wouldn't have been surprised if she'd bloodied her knuckles. As it was, her palms were an angry red.

"Where is he?" She dodged from one foot to the other, trying to look past me into my apartment. It was too early in the morning for this.

"Where's who?" I pulled open the door a little further and leaned against it but held tightly to the doorframe, blocking any chance for her to get past me. I felt a little self-conscious standing there in Ashton's Hello Kitty undies but it was still dark and I couldn't find mine.

"You know perfectly well who." Emily strained up on her toes and peered over my shoulder, then bent low and looked under my arm into the dark living room

"Aiden! " She yelled into the apartment, "Aiden! Remember what I told you I would do if you hurt him?"

"Em. Would you shut up!" I looked over my shoulder, then back at her. "He's asleep. God! Everything's fine. I'm fine. He's fine. We're all fine."

"What do you mean, *we're?*" Emily's eyebrow shot up. "Is Ashton here too?"

"Maaaaaybe." I pulled unconsciously at the briefs, remembering him slipping them off the night before. I blushed.

"What's goin' on?" She looked up, leaned forward and actually sniffed the air. "I smell sex. I can't believe it! You had another threesome, didn't you?" She had that when-will-you-ever-learn voice and it took all my will power not to roll my eyes. "Seriously!"

Em's voice has a tendency to carry. I think she knows this and uses it to her advantage. I grabbed her arm and yanked her inside. "Would you shut up?" I glanced past her for any curious neighbors before pulling the door closed.

"Well?"

"Well, what?"

"What the hell happened?"

I smiled and tilted my head feigning indignation; a hand on my chest. "I don't kiss and tell." I had to jump back to keep from getting battered by a pillow.

"This is pretty fucked up." She threw herself on the couch.

I couldn't believe she was getting mad. I mean, last time she was all; tell me everything about the whole thing, couldn't get enough and now. "Em."

"Don't Em me! I'm serious."

I don't know exactly what she saw on my face, what expression, but her eyes got big and round and she started to say something, but whatever it was, the words didn't come. She just opened her mouth to say it, and then threw her hands up in frustration. "Forget it."

"Forget what? You haven't said anything. Just made a big scene, woke the whole fucking neighborhood up and now you're acting like the world is coming to an end.."

"It is." She spoke in a whisper.

"What are you talking about? Nothing's coming to an end." I sat down next to her. "Talk to me."

"You've got *them* now." The words were mumbled into the throw pillow as she nodded towards my bedroom.

"What are you talking about?"

She leaned forward like she was about to get up. I reached for her hand and held it in both of mine. "Em. The best Em in the whole wide world; tell me what's going on in that beautiful head of yours."

That brought a little smile.

"You know how much I love you." I nudged her with my shoulder. She nodded but didn't look at me, just clasped my hand a little bit tighter.

"And no matter what happens between me and Ashton *and* Aiden, it's not going to change one thing between you and me. If anything, you better get ready for some major bitching and moaning and whining. Not to mention, story time."

She grinned. "You're just saying that to make me feel better."

"No. I'm serious. As much as I love both of them, I'm going to need you. You're my go-to girl." I stretched out on the couch and put my head in her lap. "As a matter of fact, I could use a little Em time, right now."

"Oh please! You just yelled at me and told me to go home."

"Shut up and baby me. I need pampering. Do you know how exhausting a night of hot sex can be?" She was combing her fingers through my hair, but after I said that, she smacked me on the forehead. "Ow! What was that for?"

"So… he didn't hurt you?" Serious Em was back, as if she hadn't just assaulted me.

I shook my head "No." I whined, rubbing my forehead. "But *you* did."

"You said he and Ashton were having sex."

"Well, I thought they were."

#

"What…. what were you doing out there?" It was hard to concentrate, hard to form coherent thoughts with Ashton biting at my neck.

Then again, it didn't help my concentration that Aiden had my dick in a firm grasp, massaging with both hands squeezing and pulling, a finger pressing firmly at the base. I shuddered into our kiss as he pressed himself firmly against my hip. His jeans had dropped to his ankles and he stepped out of them, prodding me rather happily with his cock. One of my hands found it's way down and I grabbed him.

Ashton was pushing me towards the bed, while working his Hello Kitty briefs down with one hand. I pulled Aiden along with us. I stopped short of falling back on the bed and Ashton actually whimpered.

Aiden leaned in against me. "We were coming to an understanding."

He pushed me firmly, my legs buckled and the three of us collapsed onto the bed. Aiden climbed on top of me. He straddled my chest and I noted the telltale scent of sex. I stared up at him, running a finger down the middle of his abs, playing with his happy trail until my hand reaches his cock again.

"An understanding?"

Aiden's nod was slow, "Uh huh." He was staring at the ceiling, his back arched, his abs tense as I played with him. He swallowed great gulps of air and the head of his cock was already slick with precum. I strained forward and licked.

I rolled my head to the left where Ashton worked with great abandon. His lips and tongue worked wondrously on my neck. He kissed me firmly, sucking on my tongue and I could taste Aiden in his mouth. I let go of Aiden's dick and reached across and grabbed Ashton's hair and pulled him into another kiss. I sucked on his tongue hungrily.

Aiden rose to his knees, still straddling me and started thrusting against me. He leaned down and found the other side of my neck and kissed it, pressing his body flush against mine: my abs slick from his dick sliding back and forth between us. The friction sent shivers through me, driving me senseless and I thrust back involuntarily.

"What? Understanding?" The words were punctuated by long drawn out kisses from Ashton.

Aiden dropped to my side, one of his legs thrown across my torso. He rutted against me as I turned towards Ashton. "That you." He bit the back of my neck. "And me." He bit again and reached around and grabbed my dick.

"And me." Ashton wrapped a hand around Aiden's and their grip tightened as they both started stroking me. I could feel Aiden's cock slipping against my asshole, each thrust a little more insistent. He was already close I could tell. His breathing had become shallow and he whimpered when he slipped past again. I reached back maneuvered him until he thrust once more and slipped inside of me. I groaned into Ashton's mouth, my own dick sliding in between Ash's legs.

I pulled Ashton tighter against me. My hand slipped down his back and to his ass. I squeezed an ass cheek as we humped each other dick to dick, his sliding up and prodding my belly button, mine teasing the underside of his balls, between his legs.

The closer Aiden came to his climax the faster and harder he thrust. It's like he couldn't get in deep enough. He lingered deep inside of me, pulled back and thrust harder, gripping my hip, pulling me to him as he lunged.

Ashton's eyes were squeezed shut. His forehead pressed against mine. The "huh huh huh" of his breath as we thrust against each other filled the room. His kisses were tentative as if he were focusing more on breathing. I slid a finger up and down his ass crack then pushed it inside of him and he shuddered. He quit thrusting, his dick pressed between us. I felt his hot wet cum shoot. He sucked the air from my mouth. I felt his abs, his entire body go rigid with his climax. He squeezed my dick between his thighs and his climax triggered my own explosion of cum.

Aiden growled, not to be outdone, he pounded into me; faster harder and deeper. I could see nothing but a burst of white each time his cock slammed against my prostate and his guttural yell was drowned out by my repeated "Oh," as I climaxed again.

I sank back against Aiden and reaching back and took his hand. "You, me and Ashton, huh?" I nodded sleepily, my heart slowing to normal. I sighed, contentedly. Ashton burrowed into my chest, with the most adorable snore.

"Okay."

~~~End of Book One~~~

137

Continue on for a SNEAK PEAK at book two of the Love & Kisses trilogy: Kiss & Tell which will be released in early 2015

CHAPTER ONE
A Friend of a Friend

Aiden

"Stay." I watched him nudge Ashton. He stirred under the sheets but pulled the blanket and pillow up over his head. Cody scowled and uncovered his face. "Ash. Tell him to stay.'

Ashton raised his head, though his eyes were still closed. He reminded me of a newborn pup looking around but unable to see yet. He grunted a little growl before burrowing up next to Cody. "See, he wants you to stay too, I could tell."

I stepped into my jeans, pulling them up, tucking carefully.

"I'm surprised you don't chafe more. That thing's so big." Cody extricated himself from Ashton and crawled to the foot of the bed.

He reached out and grabbed the zipper and pulled me towards him. "You know. I recall a little something you said to me."

"Cody I have to go. I gotta take my brothers to school."

He slipped fingers into my front pocket and pulled me more insistently. "It's still early." He smiled seductively, even going so far as to lick his lips. "Besides you owe me a blowjob."

"How do *I* owe *you* a blowjob?"

You don't remember?" He rose up on his knees and looped his arms over my shoulder. "Our first kiss. You said, and I quote 'Uhhhhh How bout this... You let me kiss you and I'll let you suck me off. Y'all like that sort of thing.'" Cody proceeded to grope me then pulled me down for a kiss.

Pulling back, I broke the kiss "As I recall, you called me an arrogant prick." I struggled to keep a smile from blossoming.

Cody feigned glee. "You *do* remember."

"You, quite literally, had me in the palm of your hand."

Cody groped me again, slipping his hands inside past the zipper. "Yeah you were playing hard to get." He gave me a quick squeeze, his smile devilish. "Not very well, but still. You promised me I could suck you off."

"Cody, seriously. I have to go." I slapped at his hands as he tried pulling my jeans down. I was starting to get hard.

"Fine." He pouted then jumped out of bed and pulled on a pair of tighty-whities. They practically glowed in the early morning darkness. He pulled on a black tank top and a pair of oversized basketball shorts. "I'm going with."

He looked back at Ashton, who was had quickly fallen fast asleep, hugging the pillow tightly against his chest. Cody jumped on the bed and kissed him, quickly. "Be back in a bit, babe."

I stared up at the ceiling. "Why exactly are you coming with me?"

I told you, I'm coming....to collect a debt."

"A debt?"

"Uh huh." He chirped. He ran into the bathroom, turning on the light and primped in front of the mirror.

I watched him for a moment before grabbing my keys and wallet off the night table. I looked down at Ashton. I couldn't help but feel a little envious. He was simply beautiful, his soft lines made even more so in sleep.

"Go on. You know you want to." I looked up startled. Cody stood in the doorway.

"Want to what?"

"Give him a kiss. It's perfectly fine."

Ashton turned on his back and sighed. I leaned down and tried to kiss him on the cheek, chaste and innocent. His eyes opened slowly and he grabbed my shirt. I started to pull away but he kissed me more insistently.

It felt weird. It's not that I didn't want to kiss him, but to be kissing him in front of Cody. It felt like cheating. I knew it wasn't. And I did want to kiss him, not just to prove that I would, like we were playing a game of spin the bottle and it just so happened to land on him, but just wanted there to be passion.

A Kiss Is Just a Kiss

While we had come to an understanding concerning our relationship with Cody, Ashton and I still hadn't come to an understanding as to what *our* relationship might be.

Chaste kissing and the occasional threesome was the bulk of our relationship. We'd talk in passing in the morning, small talk over the breakfast table. The three of us would snuggle on the couch during a movie. There was no real flirting, no furtive glances, no passing touches. Most of our interaction was mechanical, like we were an old married couple going through the motions, the passion gone, except in this case, the passion had yet to be ignited.

I couldn't help but recall our initial encounters; before Cody and I ever crossed paths.

I'd gotten Ashton's number from a *friend.* We met at a coffee shop on the other side of town. I was petrified that someone would see me, recognize me, or worse, recognize Ashton and know what he did and then everyone would know. I followed him to his apartment talking to myself the whole way, telling myself how crazy I was being. Every exit beckoned me to turn away, to stop the nonsense. I don't know what need drove me, forced me to keep going. I sat in the car for a long moment, the engine ticking while Ashton stood in the doorway, the light from his apartment casting his shadow.

Kissing Ashton then, my whole body shook with anticipation, with trepidation. When he stripped down to nothing but a pair of batman underwear I'd lost my breath, and then he slowly undressed me, every incidental touch, against my chest, my abs, or along my thigh as he lowered my jeans, was electric. He told me to take his underwear off and my hands shook, touching him, my touch so tentative, my heart pounding and in that moment I was never so scared of what was coming. Then he pushed me back onto his bed and kissed me; a kiss so intimate, but so foreign.

I shuddered. I'd forgotten all about that. So much had happened since. I was not that boy hiding behind a façade of bravado. Not anymore.

CHAPTER TWO
A Little Heads Up

"You're kidding, right?"

I looked over at Cody. His boss had called from the bookstore.

"I'm with my boyfriend." He held the phone away from his ear and mimicked her talking. Then pulled it back to his ear. "But I'm.... I'm not ....I'm not even dressed for work. What? I know, but... Fine... No, I'll get Aiden to drop me off... Well it's too late for that...no...no... I don't mind."

I could tell he was getting frustrated. I reached over and took his free hand and squeezed it.

"Elaine, I said I'd come, so...it's fine... Give me like 20 minutes and I'll be there." Cody tossed his phone on the dashboard. "Well, shit!"

"What happened?"

Cody shook his head. "This new kid she hired last week, quit. Her nephew. If he wasn't so fucking cute, I'd be glad he was gone. He didn't do shit, anyways. It's okay if you dropped me off?" He still held my hand and he kissed it, giving me his best puppy dog eyes.

"Cute, huh?"

Cody nodded. "An ass to die for." He had an evil smirk. "You're not jealous, are you?"

I looked straight ahead, pretending to pay attention to the traffic. I guess it would appear more realistic if there was more traffic.

"Awww, my poor bae. Don't be jelly." He let go of my hand and unbuckled his seatbelt. He maneuvered in the seat until he was on his knees. He leaned over, whispering in my ear. "You're ass is way better than his, any day."

I couldn't help but smile, but tilted my head away from him anyway. "Yeah, yeah, whatever."

"You know, I have the store for a whole hour before we open." He kissed my neck. He worked his lips to dizzying affect. "I can show you just how much I appreciate your ass. I can give you a tour." He kissed my neck, once twice three times. "Show you the backroom." His breath was warm on my neck and his tongue trailed up from my collarbone.

"What is it with you this morning?" I tried pushing him away, though my efforts weren't a hundred percent.

"Hey! Ten and two o'clock mister." He growled, slapping my hand away.

I gripped the steering wheel as he continued to play his tongue along my collarbone. "You're gonna make me wreck."

"You just pay attention to the road." His voice was seductive, almost commanding.

"Cody." I was trapped as his hands rubbed up and down my chest, stopping only to pinch my nipples until they were hard.

He lifted my shirt and started fiddling with my jeans.

"What are you doing?"

"I told you. I'm collecting a debt." His eyes were intense; mesmerizing, and his lips glistened.

"Now?" I felt the zipper give way, a loosening around my waist. "I don't think..." And that was all I could say as he reached in and pulled me free. While verbally I objected to this dangerous activity, still I reached down and adjusted my seat back, then quickly gripped the wheel again. *This was not safe. Not safe at all.* But my brain was quickly overruled. I cast quick furtive glances down. I was hard in a matter of seconds, milliseconds, and all I could do was gasp as he bobbed up and down on my cock. At one point I started to close my eyes then remembered where I was. A blaring horn made me realize I had slowed to 30 miles an hour on the freeway.

He held my cock at the base; his pinky finger playing with my balls. His left hand played up under my shirt, pinching my hard nipples. He laid his head on my lap and licked my sensitive head. I shivered as he stared up at me, the head of my cock in the kiss of his lips. My hips were thrusting on their own accord. I wanted my cock back in the warmth of his mouth. It glistened from the spit.

His teeth scraped across my dickhead. I leaned back hard in the seat and hissed. "Shit!" Another horn blared as I swerved the car. "Cody, you gotta stop." I panted, trying to pull him off of me. Instead of stopping, he went all the way down on me. I gasped as he sucked me hard. My jaw ached; it was clenched so hard. It took all my concentration to stay on the road. "Cody. Cody. Co...." The last part of his name was lost in a gasp.

I came convulsively, my hips thrusting, a hand on the back of his head, fingers gripping his hair; holding him there as I unloaded. My grip on the steering wheel left my knuckles white.

Afterwards Cody rose up, wiping his mouth with his arm. . His lips were so red; they looked bloody. He didn't say anything as he sat back. He looked in the mirror, fixed his hair, rubbed a little cum off his cheek. He fidgeted with the stereo, pushing buttons randomly but found nothing of interest. He played with the windows, rolling them down, then up. He adjusted the side mirror then leaned down and looked at the traffic behind us.

"What's the matter? Did I hurt you?"

Cody looked back at me, shaking his head. "No." He looked like he wanted to say more but looked back out the window instead.

"Are you sure?"

He nodded but didn't say anything.

"Cody." I tried again.

"I'm fine" He rolled the windows down again and flew his hand up and down on the draft.

"You don't seem fine. One minute you're all over me. Now you're not even looking at me." The wind drowned out my voice.

He rolled the window up, the silence deafening. "I don't know why I did that. I mean, I do, but..." Cody smacked his lips then looked over at me. "Can you go through a drive-thru. I need something to drink."

"Yeah, sure. You want McDonald's?"

"It doesn't matter. Just something to wash the taste out of my mouth. Plus, I don't want to be at work with cum breath." He cringed. "That sounded rude."

"Cody, what's the matter?"

"Huh?"

"Something's wrong?" I pulled off the freeway and aimed for the golden arches. My imagination was getting the better of me. I could almost taste their French fries.

"It's nothing. I was just looking forward to spending the day with you."

I smirked. "Well that, I can see."

"Jerk." He smacked me on the shoulder. "For that, you're buying my Dr. Pepper and I want a Big Mac and fries."

"Hey! You said it, I was just agreeing with you." I rubbed my shoulder.

"And no cheese."

"Yes dear."

We ate in the car, in front of the store. I stole some of his fries and he only growled twice.

"You gonna pick me up?" He talked through a mouthful of burger. "I'm probably gonna be here till like two, then Ben comes in."

I clapped my hands against the steering wheel. "Then I'll be here waiting. With bells on."

"Bells, huh? Anything else?"

"Nope, just bells. Big bells. And if you're lucky, I'll let you ring 'em."

"Tease." He stuffed his trash into the McDonald's bag. "Okay." He leaned over and gave me a kiss. I could taste special sauce on his lips. "I'll see you at 2:00."

I watched him unlock the door to the bookstore and relock it from the inside. He smiled and kissed the window then wiped his kiss off the glass. He waved quickly, and then disappeared into the store.

I sat for a minute. His smile had put me at ease but I wondered about his moment of melancholy, wondered what he was about to say before he changed the subject.

Nicholas Scott

Kiss & Tell
Coming in 2015

Available Now
Bright Light Black Rainbows
(A Fairweather High novel)
Just One Bite
Book One of the Edge of Night trilogy

KISS
&
TELL

a Love & Kisses Novel

Nicholas Scott

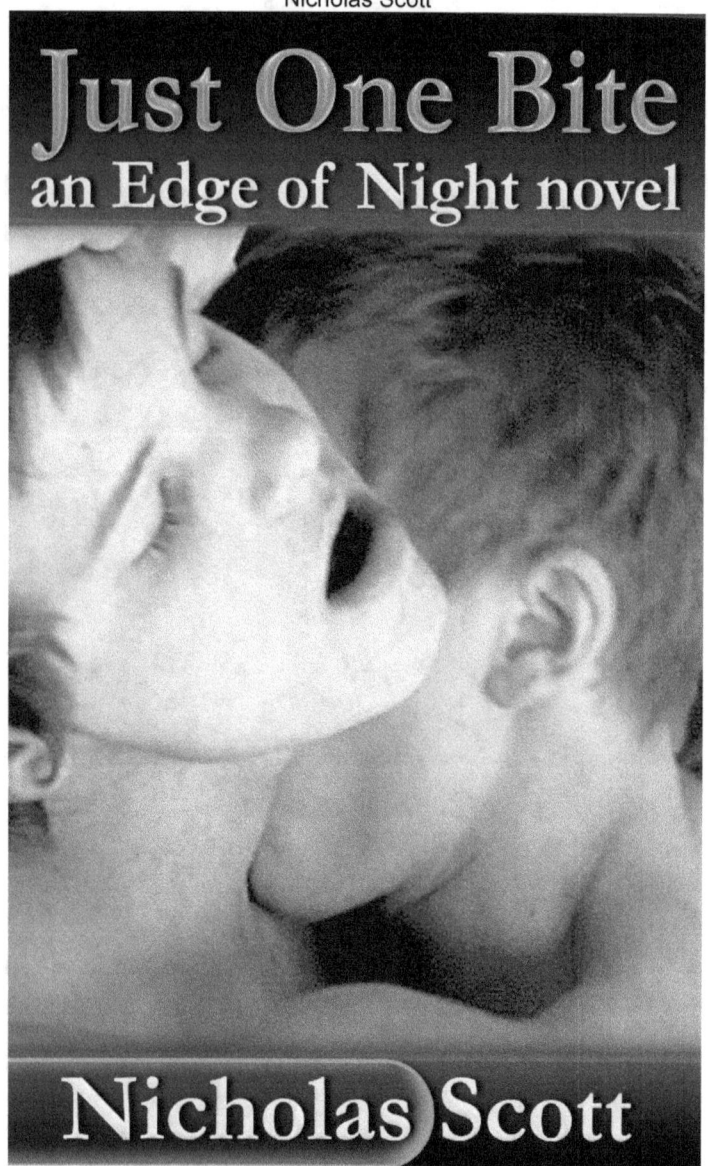